G R JORDAN

Fair Market Value

A Highlands and Islands Detective Thriller

First published by Carpetless Publishing 2021

First edition

ISBN: 978-1-914073-39-7

This book was professionally typeset on Reedsy.
Find out more at reedsy.com

Nothing will teach you more about perceived value than taking something with literally no value and selling it in the auction format. It teaches you the beauty and power of presentation, and how you can make magic out of nothing.

Sophia Amoruso

Contents

Foreword

This story is set in the north of Scotland based around a fictional auction house in Invershin. Although incorporating known cities, towns and villages, note that all events, persons, structures and specific places are fictional and not to be confused with actual buildings and structures which have been used as an inspirational canvas to tell a completely fictional story.

And as far as I'm aware there is no secret society with a religious twist, led by a Scottish landowner and hunting down powerful relics to use for the betterment of the world at large. I could be wrong...

Acknowledgement

To Susan, Jean and Rosemary for your work in bringing this novel to completion, your time and effort is deeply appreciated.

Chapter 01

Annie was proud of herself. After several years of being in and out of rehab due to the damn drugs that plagued her life, she had turned a corner at what she was now appreciating as the tender age of fifty-six. She now had her first job in over fifteen years—well, at least her first job that was not illegal in some fashion. Before, she had always scraped by, making her way by working for dubious men or women in schemes that paid for the next jag in her arm. But a close friend had helped her until she had started to get herself sorted. The clinic and the rehab had brought her to a point where, while she could not say she never thought about drugs, she certainly had an attitude of not wanting to take any.

Her mind these days was lucid. There was less apprehension and tension, fewer cold sweats at night. Was she finally clear? Oh, never. There was always that haunting shadow coming over the back, that worrying feeling that at any point, you could suddenly crash. It wasn't the high she remembered; it was those gutting lows. But maybe that was a good thing; maybe that was what kept her off it.

The bus was winding its way along through the lush highland countryside; the green mountainside, tinged with heather, looked like a simple rock covered in moss, but when you focused clearly, you saw the individual bushes, trees, and wild grass that made up the abundant textures of what was her home. Just by the road, the River Shin coursed, cutting a deep channel and providing a pleasant backdrop to the simple journey to her new place of work.

She had never seen herself working in an auction showroom, but then again, she was only cleaning. The last few days, which coincidentally had been her first few days of work, had been a flurry of activity and Annie had stared at wonder at the various exhibits that were piled in the back of the showroom. She could not tell what was precious from what was simply junk and surely, like most of these places, some of it must have been junk.

She had watched the programmes on TV, always with a man or woman rather eloquently, if somewhat eccentrically, dressed, usually with a pair of those glasses that only had half-lenses in them, and if it was a man, certainly some sort of pocket watch hanging from a smart waistcoat. There were always two teams or some sort of competition about who could sell for the most, and Annie dreamt of this happening in this auction house, thinking about herself being one of the contestants. She would need somebody useful with her and, no doubt, she would always listen to the expert, going along with that advice, for she knew next to nothing when it came to antiques.

She had not been allowed to clean any of the items; her job was only to clean around them, make sure the floors, toilets, and all other parts looked immaculate for the opening day. The owner, Mr. Mackenzie, had said she could come along, watch from the back, but obviously, not to wear the pinny they were giving her. When she had turned up, he had given her a quick wink, told her the place looked great, obviously happy with her work. He had been busy though and had not stopped to chat. She remembered seeing him up at the front, gavel in hand, bringing it down on item after item.

There was also an internet link and Annie was never quite sure just exactly how this worked. Was it really live? Mackenzie's head was constantly flicking back and forward from the auction room floor to a screen beside him, and several bids went online. There was that moment when he seemed a little bit apprehensive as if something had gone wrong on the internet. But, overall, the day had gone smoothly and when she had left, knowing she would be back in in the morning to help clear up, Annie had seen a happy Mr. Mackenzie.

She liked that. A happy boss tended to be a good boss, one who was generous to his workers. Not that Annie was looking for any special compensation. She did her work, and she did it well. Her fear did not come from a lack of skill at keeping the place spotless, her fear came from when she left work. Would she blow it by finding another one of those seedy vendors? The ones who enticed you and wanted to keep you coming back for more of their wares.

As Annie stepped off the bus, she looked at the new building before her. The car park was still only gravel. Mr. Mackenzie said they would be tarmacking it at some point but, for now, it would have to do until they could realise more funds. Annie thought it was rather a strange place, the auction house placed aside the River Shin away from everything but, then again, maybe it was a day out for people. After all, auction houses weren't something you popped into like the supermarket; you went to them for a day, a chance to dream about owning something, the excitement of the bidding.

The front of the building had a bright new sign, Mackenzie Auctioneers. It was rather dashing, red and rich blue, with a lettering so ornate it almost looked like an antique itself. But inside, the facilities were very modern, from the rows of seats that she had laid out to the white-walled viewing room that had been busy for the two days before. It had a thick carpet on its floor, which Mr. Mackenzie said was there to make a homelier feel. The building was modern and kept the heat despite running on a very low-energy consumption. And yet the building still looked homely, if a little bit old-worldly. The carpet had to be cleaned and after the first day's viewing, Annie worked hard to get a deep stain out of the rich, red carpet in the viewing room. Still, these things were bound to happen.

Annie made her way across the car park and saw only one car there. She recognized it as Mr. Mackenzie's and thought he must be in early. She took a quick glance at her watch. 09:00, bang-on. Well, he wouldn't think she was late anyway. She approached the side door, rather than try the large ones at the front where the public would normally enter. The rear door was double glazed with a simple lock that she had a key for. She pressed down on the handle but found the door locked and thought that was unusual because Mr. Mackenzie usually came in the side door when he was coming to work on a normal office day. She doubted the front doors would be open until the public were allowed access. Of course, that would not be today. This was a recovery day, a day to get the place clean again before he set up for the next auction.

Taking her key, Annie opened the door and stepped inside onto the simple wooden floor that was a trademark of the rear offices.

'Mr. Mackenzie, Mr. Mackenzie, it's just Annie. I'll just get

4

the pinny on and get to it. Is there anywhere in particular you want me to do first?'

No reply came and Annie thought he must have earphones in or some other sort of distraction going on, so she made her way along the corridor to her cleaning cupboard. Inside, she found her pinny and dressed herself accordingly before taking out a mop and bucket. The front entrance had a tiled area before the opening into the main auction hall, and after yesterday, it would be as dirty as anything, so many feet trampling over it. She'd start there, then she'd come inside and begin the tidy up. She'd need to hoover and dust everything down.

Annie anticipated being here for the day and when she checked her buses, she thought today she could get the half past five, rather than the normal quarter past four she usually got. Of course, most days, she didn't come in until the afternoon either, but Mr. Mackenzie said today would be busy, plenty to do, so Annie was prepared.

Making her way with the mop and bucket, Annie walked through the back corridor and made her way into the small kitchen area which had a low tap at the rear. She filled up her bucket with water and then walked along the wooden corridor, shouting again for Mr. Mackenzie. She had to reverse into the main auction hall, pushing open the doors with her backside as she carried the mop bucket through. Her eyes ran along one side of the auction hall which held pictures, most of which weren't that expensive, but instead showed auctioneers in action. Annie smiled looking at them. Her eyes continued to focus on them as she wandered along and out to the front.

The internal double doors that entered into the main auction hall were open and she saw the tiled area ahead of her. Placing her bucket down, she dipped her mop in, started to mop up, and

5

made her way across the tiled floor. There was plenty of dirt but she'd soon have it pristine. A small patch of the tiles made their way underneath the very front doors and Annie realized she'd have to open them to clean it thoroughly. She reached for her key, put it into the lock, turned it but realized that the doors were unlocked. Someone must have opened the doors already today, so pressing down on the handles, Annie opened both doors wide. *Maybe the boss came in this way*, thought Annie, *although that's unusual.*

Annie had a job to do and so continued with cleaning the floor, sweeping this way and that with the mop before getting to a point where it was all clean and she had now backed herself into the main auction hall. There were a few windows and skylights that let light in but, in truth, the main auction hall was fairly dark. Yesterday all the lights had been on when it had been in full throttle and there had been that buzzing murmur of people anxiously checking bids and looking through brochures at items that were about to come up.

But now, it was quiet as Annie turned around and looked into the auction hall fully for the first time since she'd arrived. She had entered and looked at the sidewall on her way up to the front door. Now, as she stared into the main room, she was glad she had. The chairs, which had been neatly arranged in rows the day before, were all higgledy-piggledy where people had stood up, bumped, and moved around, but it wasn't their disorder that caught her eye. Instead, as she looked on the stage, she saw the podium area, the place where Mr. Mackenzie would stand with his gavel, the screens to the left-hand side.

Yesterday, you could see him from about mid-chest up and he'd lean forward enticing the audience, whipping them up, driving up the bids for each item as best he could. Now, he was still on the podium, but he was slumped over the front, the top of his head pointing toward her. In the darkness of the room, it looked like he had some sort of small hat on, like something a Jewish man would wear. Annie made her way across the hall, wondering if the man had simply drunk too much. *Had he been in here reliving yesterday's glory, six sheets to the wind, and then collapsed and slept over the podium?*

'Mr. Mackenzie, time to get up, sir. Mr. Mackenzie, come on. I'll get you a couple of paracetamol; you can sit down in the office. Don't blame you for celebrating. Good day, yesterday. You must have taken some serious money.'

As Annie got closer, something inside her began to become uneasy. Mr. Mackenzie was not moving. His body should be doing something, even if he were just breathing, it would rise and fall somewhere. His right arm was hung over the front, but his left arm was in what seemed like an impossible angle. *It shouldn't bend like that.* Annie ran forward, up onto the platform, and as she made her way across quickly, she lost her footing, sliding on a wet floor. As she went to pick herself up, she realized that the wet was on her hands and as she looked at it in the dim light, she thought it to be dark and red.

Looking up at Mackenzie, she saw his legs, one braced out in a bizarre fashion, the foot slightly off the floor. She stood up quickly, her heart now thumping, and Annie reached for the man's shoulders to find them cold to the touch. She went to try and move him backwards but he was rigid. As she leaned closer, she saw the back of his head was caved in, a mass of blood and possibly brain, or maybe it was bone as well.

She screamed, stumbled backwards for there was something else sitting inside the man's head. She reached up, almost an instinct, to grab it and pull it out. The item was small, wooden and as she fell backwards with it in her hands, Annie saw a gavel, the one Mr. Mackenzie would use to signify that the bidding had closed.

Annie shuffled backwards and hit the rear wall of the platform. She looked up at Mr. Mackenzie's back and legs. The man was dead. Annie had seen dead bodies before. Friends who had overdosed, had passed on from the drugs but this was different. She turned and looked at the object in her hand. The wooden gavel had blood on it, and other bits that she didn't want to identify. Her eyes shot from it back to Mackenzie, and then back to it again. *Oh God*, she thought. *Oh, God*. The bidding for Mr. Mackenzie had definitely closed.

Chapter 02

'**N**o.'
'You can't just say no, Seoras; you have to give me a reason.' Hope stared across the table at her boss. He had his head down, sitting in his chair with a cup of coffee in front of him. The papers he had been holding, which contained a number of names—potential candidates for joining the team—had been jettisoned onto the table and the engagement that Macleod had shown moments before was gone.

'I can say no and I said no. Look at them. No.'

'There's nothing wrong with these officers,' said Hope. 'They're all perfectly good. They would be useful. They could replace Kirsten.'

'They could come in and take a wage, but they certainly could not replace Kirsten. Look at them. There isn't any of them there that's got her ability to see through things, never mind be able to handle all the data she used to get through.'

'There's plenty of data handlers in there,' said Hope. 'Look, I get it. You lost your favourite.' Hope saw Macleod's head raised and his eyes stared at her. 'Okay, not your favourite, one of your favourites. Someone you really liked, cherished, and thought was really good at her job. Okay? I didn't mean favourite. You don't do favourites.'

Macleod dropped his head and settled back down to staring at his coffee. 'I'm glad you cleared that up,' he said. 'Of course, they're useful police officers. Of course, they could do a job but they're not Kirsten. This team was tight. This team had reached a level. We need somebody special to fill that gap.'

'And it's been four weeks,' said Hope. 'Four weeks of looking at names and candidates. When are you going to make a move? We're just lucky there hasn't been a proper investigation going on.'

'Well, I've been working,' said Macleod 'And we've managed, the three of us.'

'We've managed because there hasn't been a proper investigation. The two bodies they found underneath the rubble. I mean, that was ancient history. Check through records. See who had disappeared, a couple of hobos in the ground. That was not a murder investigation. We haven't been stretched with anything that's tested us. We've been pretty fortunate.'

'She was special. You know that, don't you?'

'I know you really thought a lot of Kirsten as a person. You realise Jane tells me you keep disappearing out at night. You're lucky she's not a suspicious woman thinking you're off with some floozy somewhere.' Macleod's eyes flashed up again. 'I know where you've been going,' said Hope. 'I'm sure Kirsten would appreciate it. Does her brother appreciate it?'

'Her brother doesn't know who I am. He doesn't know who Kirsten is when I show him the photograph. No recollection. He's well. He's okay. He's fit. He's healthy. They look after him but he doesn't know what's going on, who's who. He gets confused. At one point I showed him my warrant card to someone, and he panicked. He thought I was there to arrest him. It's a sad end. She was really close to him.'

'She's off doing other things, what she wanted, what you told her to do,' said Hope. 'Can we get on and do what we're meant to do and get someone else into this team?'

'Of course, we can,' said Macleod, picking up his coffee and drinking the last of it. 'Just get me some names that I can actually employ. Not these fine, but evidently unsuitable, officers.'

'Oh, so delicately put,' said Hope. She shook her head and stood up to leave the office in disgust.

'I don't appreciate that tone,' shouted Macleod after her and stood up from the side table where he held his briefings to make his way to the window at the rear of the Inverness Police Station. He needed to pick someone, he knew that, but he wanted the best. He remembered back to when he'd found Kirsten. A police officer working uniform on the Isle of Lewis. She'd helped him greatly in a murder of an American man and his wife. Then she had become part of the furniture, but it seemed that furniture was easier to change when it was the wooden kind. When it was people, it was much harder to let go.

There came a knock at the office door and when it opened before he could say anything, he knew it was Hope. Hope McGrath had been with Detective Inspector Macleod longer than anyone on the team and had been a challenge when they'd first found each other, working in an unlikely partnership. But she knew him now and he knew her. It was his desire that one day she'd move up the ranks to where he was.

'Seoras,' said Hope, using his first name. 'They've found someone. Bad way.'

Macleod spun round. 'Who, in what way?'

'A Forrest Mackenzie, sir, an auctioneer, back of the head

11

smashed in. Gavel left inside. Looks more than a straightfor-
ward murder, possibly other things involved. Definite message
has been sent there.'

'Well then, I guess this short-handed team is going to have
to go and work out who did it.' Macleod grabbed his coat, saw
the sergeant turn on her heel and shout over to Ross. He was
working at a computer in the far corner of the outer office.

DC Ross had been on the team almost as long as Hope had and
was an incredibly amiable fellow but was also someone who was
very, very thorough. He was able to pick up all the loose ends
around the cases, able to make sure all the basic logistics were
covered. This suited Macleod because that was far from his
forte. Macleod's strength was solving crimes, understanding
the individuals and Hope was his little terrier that charged
around in front of him digging things up. Of course, he never
told her the way he imagined the team in his mind.

The auction house at Invershin was north of Inverness and
the drive took almost an hour to get there. Not that Macleod
was complaining as Hope drove along because he loved this
part of the world, the lushness of the mountainsides, the fresh
air, and the beauty when the sun shone near the loch-sides
that you passed. How the rivers gleamed while everywhere
seemed a mile away from the big city. He'd spent twenty years
in Glasgow after being brought up on the Isle of Lewis, and as
much as he had been successful at his job in the city, he longed
for the quieter areas, and here in the Highlands, he'd found
another home.

Hope pulled up into the gravel car park, a small amount of
dust rising as she applied the brakes. Macleod looked around
to see a forensic van already there and a number of uniformed
officers milling about. He saw stares of recognition as he exited

the car.

'Inspector,' shouted a uniformed sergeant, 'Glad you're here. To bring you up to date, Ms. Nakamura is here with her forensic team. She's only just gone in. The woman who found the body of Mr. Forrest Mackenzie is a cleaner by the name of Annie Gilmartin. She was due to come in and clean this morning and was surprised when Mr. Mackenzie was actually in the building. She saw his car outside. One thing she did say, though, was it had been a terribly busy day yesterday. This is a new auction house. It was their first auction yesterday, and they'd been getting ready for it all week. There's only a couple of other staff, and the first of the officers have intercepted them. It appears at the moment that Mr. Mackenzie was the main organizer of the event. The other staff have only been employed for a couple of weeks. It looks very much like a one-man show.'

'How's Annie Gilmartin taking it?' asked Macleod.

'Not well. Apparently, she was quite a druggie, a user who's got herself back off the drugs, so there's a little bit of a worry about her with the shock that this has caused. She has a partner. We've got word to her and she's coming up, but I've left one of our uniformed officers with Annie in the back, getting her a cup of tea, and that. It wasn't pleasant, the body, sir.'

'Yes, bodies rarely are, Sergeant, but thank you. Keep a perimeter as you're probably going to get some press arrive. I don't want them in the car park. Keep them well back, and nobody goes into any of these rooms until Ms. Nakamura is happy.'

'Of course,' said the sergeant.

Macleod heard a second car pull up in the car park, and saw Ross getting out of it.

'And Sergeant,' said Macleod, 'A car's just pulled up. That's

D.C. Ross. Liaise with him. He's going to be going into the records of the place, so he'll need to have a good idea about what's happening, where this company comes from, anything you can feed towards him in that respect. He might need a few bodies as well to do a bit of checking and that.'

'Of course, Inspector. Not a problem.'

'Shall we go and see Jona?' asked Hope.

'We'll pay her a quick visit,' said Macleod, 'Then we'll talk to Annie Gilmartin.' Macleod made his way over to the forensic vehicle and was handed a set of white overalls. Once he'd donned them and put the plastic onto his shoes, he and Hope entered the auction house, carefully avoiding any markers on the floor put down by the forensic team. Jona Nakamura was up on the platform of the main auction hall, staring at the man slumped over a podium.

'Beat you to it, Inspector. What's kept you?'

Jona Nakamura was the Senior Forensic Officer at Inverness Police Station. Over the last year or two, she'd developed a closeness with Macleod, to such a point that they actually would have meditation sessions together. The young Asian woman was attractive, but what really got to Macleod about her was her ability to help him ease away the darkness that came with his job. There was a level of understanding between them that was deeper than even he and Hope had. His Glaswegian sergeant could never have the same understanding of him like Jona Nakamura had, and sometimes he found it a little discomforting just how well he and Jona clicked.

'You can't blame me for how slow Hope drives,' said Macleod, and heard a little yelp of complaint from behind him.

'Well, you'd better get up and have a look at this,' said Jona. 'This is Forrest Mackenzie, the owner of the establishment.

He's been dead at least since last night. The body's gone stiff, and he's got a large hole in the back of his head. Apparently, there was a gavel inside it. Said gavel is over there in a bag, on the floor. We'll be running it for fingerprints, et cetera, but unfortunately, Annie Gilmartin has picked it up. She approached from behind the victim when she saw him up here and then managed to take the gavel out. I believe she thought she could help him, save him somehow.'

'But it didn't have any effect, did it?' said Hope.

'No,' said Jona, 'Long gone. He's been dead, like I said, since the previous night, and it's going to be a job to get him off this podium the way he's wrapped round it, but I will do, and I'll get him back to the mortuary and find out what I can about him. However, on a first look, I would say the gavel certainly wasn't the murder weapon even if Annie did see it inside the man's head.'

'So, what was?' asked Macleod.

'Something very heavy, and I don't think it was done here,' said Jona. 'A kind of high-impact blow to the back of a head, one that's going to smash a skull in, and going to cause blood everywhere. There is some blood here, but nothing like I would expect. I think he was killed elsewhere, bludgeoned, and then I think they brought him here. They stuck the gavel in the back of his head.'

'You think they were making a point?' asked Macleod.

'I didn't say that. I tell you what happened. I tell you how they found the body. You tell me why they did it.'

'Somebody sending a message,' said Hope. 'But why?'

'Well,' said Macleod, 'they said this was the first auction here. We need to look at that first auction. Annie said it was successful according to the sergeant outside. She was here to clear up. Was there something in that auction? Was there something wrong? How did he pay for this building? Apparently, he was some sort of one-man band. Where's his funding come from? All this sort of thing. Need to get Ross on to that, Hope.'

'And what's his history?' asked Hope. 'Where's he come from before this? Maybe it's somebody coming after him from earlier on. Maybe he left debts behind.'

'You get any more, you tell me what's the deal,' said Macleod to Jona and watched as the Asian woman smiled.

'Did it all go okay last night?' she said.

Macleod had a session with Jona where they both sat motionless in his living room before talking through gently about how they were feeling about life. Afterwards, he'd gone off to visit Kirsten Stewart's brother. He'd been feeling guilty that her brother did not get to see Kirsten anymore, even if he did not remember her. Macleod had encouraged her to join the secret services. Kirsten was now dispatched to various parts of the country most of which she didn't know she would be going to until the last moment. She operated so much in the dark. For years before, while she'd been on his team, she had cared for her brother but his mental health had deteriorated and now he had a form of dementia where he knew no one. Kirsten was barely able to visit, so Macleod felt it was on him to do it.

'It went fine, Jona.'

With that dour statement, Macleod left the auction hall with Hope to stand outside in the car park. He pulled down his white hood, breathed in the fresh Scottish air.

'He picked a nice place for it,' said Hope. 'Falls of Shin up ahead. I mean, they're gorgeous. Decent tourist route coming through. I wonder if he was going to set up a little shop or something.'

'How do these places make money? I mean, right here in Invershin, it's not exactly a hive for antiques, is it?' asked Macleod.

'I don't know,' said Hope. 'Jona would probably know, well, her grandfather, at least; you know he's into antiques and all that.'

'Well, we better start becoming experts,' said Macleod, 'because this looks like it was done for a reason. Done as some sort of revenge, a warning, or some sort of score being settled. We are going to need to immerse ourselves in this world. It's going to take more than a couple of episodes of *Bargain Hunt* to make that happen.'

Chapter 03

Macleod sat on the bonnet of his car, skimming through brochures of the auction house. They were of yesterday's sale, all the items listed in the catalogue, giving a rough estimation and a brief detail of the history. Macleod, however, was struggling. At first, he thought he'd try and pick out the most expensive items and see if they would ring any bells as to why someone would want to murder the auctioneer.

Nothing was forthcoming, apart from a mind-blowing thought that some of this junk, as Macleod thought of it, was worth so much. Most of what he looked at he thought of as rubbish. In a moment, he would interview Annie Gilmartin, the cleaner who had found the body.

The woman was in quite a state. He was letting her calm down because he thought there was extraordinarily little about the immediate finding of the body that would shed any light. Rather, he wanted to get the woman's impressions over the last week that she had been employed, and see if he could under-stand Forrest Mackenzie, the dead man, from her observations.

Macleod was also waiting for Jona Nakamura. He had asked for a few moments from her over half an hour ago. She said she'd been busy and would get to him as soon as she could. During one case on the Isle of Barra, Jona's grandfather had been extremely useful, recognizing a piece of art that Macleod had no idea about. He wondered if this would be an ideal route, possibly sending the man the brochure. The more and more he looked through the photographed items, it was dawning on him that he was very out of his depth.

There were two lines of inquiry; there would be the antiques, but there will also be the people. Macleod had already started to get Ross to look into the background of Forrest Mackenzie and his constable was in one of the back offices of the auction house typing away on his laptop.

'Inspector, you said you wanted a moment' called Jona Nakamura, still dressed in her white coveralls. She pulled her hood back and let her long black hair hang out the back for a moment. 'It's always warm under these suits. It sure is always warm. You feel like you could do with a shower the moment you put them on.'

He watched her reach back and take the hair tie off her hair and shake her hair out. Macleod had always wondered how she'd never had a boyfriend. Maybe she was just above it all, happy as she was, but it certainly couldn't have been from a lack of male engagement. No, he should get with it; maybe there was a lack of female engagement. That was the thing about nowadays, you could not be too close minded. He'd had to change his way of thinking about things. Change standards which had been drummed into him when he was young. Sins of this, sins of that. Nowadays required a more live-and-let-live attitude. Working on the murder squad made that attitude somewhat ironic.

'Looking through the brochure, Jona, I can't make head

19

nor tail of the importance of these items. Before on Barra, you helped us, or rather your grandfather helped us. I was wondering if we could do the same with this case. He's quite into his antiques and that, isn't he?'

'Grandfather is into antiques, but I think he could be struggling here. It's a wide breadth and range you've got. Give me the brochure a minute.'

Jona took the brochure and started flicking through it. Every now and again she would stop, staring intently at one item or another and then continuing her search through the pamphlet.

'I think you'd be out of luck with Grandfather, Inspector. It's too wide a breadth. He knows a lot about certain types of antiques. There's so much here. You need an expert and I mean a proper expert as I'm out of my depth as well.'

'I've asked Ross to start looking through the items. I wanted him to try and pull out a few things, some of the more impressive ones.'

'Well, I don't know about that,' said Jona. 'That's a tall order for him. You really need some help here. If I was you I'd go and talk to him about it.'

Macleod nodded his thanks to Jona who promptly put her hair tie back on, pulled the hood up of her suit, and walked back inside the building. She was a stickler for detail and duty. Macleod knew he would have his reports soon enough. Right now, he'd need to talk things over with Ross. See how he was getting on and then go and interview his only witness.

Macleod walked around the side of the main building, entering through the side door, the one that Annie Gilmartin had taken earlier on in that day. The Inspector located his constable sitting behind a wooden desk in a room with white walls, filing cabinets, and a small window letting the daylight shine through.

'Did you deliberately pick the most boring room going?' asked Macleod.

'It's quiet, sir. At the end of the day, that's what's important. I need a bit of peace and quiet to work.'

'Okay, hint taken then,' said Macleod, and he watched Ross jump as if he had offended the Inspector. 'No, no, it's okay. I'm just joking with you.'

'It's a bit unsettling, sir. You don't tend to joke much.'

This was true. Macleod was not one for joking. Ever since they'd broken down the old standards of sir and ma'am, he had tried to become more of a touchy-feely Inspector. Hope thought that he was failing miserably at it. He reckoned that was just a stick to help drive him on.

'How is the search going with regard the antiques?' He saw Ross drop his eyes and sigh.

'Look, it's just, I'm not particularly good at this sort of thing. Well, not with this. I'm looking at these items and I have no idea what's important and what isn't. I really haven't got a clue. I started going into the background of Forrest Mackenzie and tracing back where he came from. These items, sir. I'm at a loss. Did you try Jona? Her grandfather's quite good in these things.'

Macleod nodded, 'I tried Jona and Jona said no. She said it's too wide a field, not specialist enough. Said we need a real expert.'

'If it's an expert we need, I might have somebody,' said Ross. 'The sergeant I worked with on the last case, the one that I took with me to Lord Argyle's house, she was able to pick out a lot of art work by just looking at it. She could be your woman. I've worked with her and she's good. Thorough. Possibly a little bit ostentatious for yourself, sir'.

'What's that meant to mean?'

'Well, she's a wee bit flamboyant, shall we say.'

'Did she break the rules, Ross?'

'No, sir. Not at all. Very clever with it though.'

'Urquhart, wasn't it? Sergeant Urquhart, if I remember right. What's she doing now, Ross? Do you know?'

'No, sir. Shall I find out?'

'Yes. Find out. Let me know. If you think she's good enough, let's get her in on this.' Ross nodded and Macleod left the small room, keen to let Ross get back to his hunting through the internet. As Macleod turned a corner, he bumped into Hope. In contrast to Macleod's shirt and tie, trousers, and jacket, Hope stood in boots, jeans, and a t-shirt. Macleod always thought that standards had gone down, but he'd find with Hope that she was able to carry even the simplest and least formal sense of clothing. Her red hair would have caught any man's eye, but nowadays she had a scar across one side of her face, a remnant from saving the life of Macleod's partner. In contrast to the early days, when he found her difficult to stare at without thinking of her as a woman to be with, nowadays he saw a police partner, a pillar that held him up—in fact, a foil for his errors and a fine police officer.

'You ready for Gilmartin, sir? She's just through the door over there. Pretty shaken up.'

'Yes, Hope, let's go through. See what the woman knows.'

'Just be advised, sir, she was a junkie, so I'm not sure how much we can trust what she's saying.'

'Is she straight now? I mean, she hasn't taken anything recently, has she?'

'No, sir. There's also a Samantha in with her at the moment.

That's her partner. I didn't know if you'd want her in with her.'

'Is she calming the woman?' asked Macleod.

'I'd say so.'

'Then she stays; this Annie Gilmartin doesn't seem to be a suspect. The uniforms have already confirmed that she was on the bus this morning coming in. She was on the bus last night before Gilmartin had left, or at least before everybody else had left. It's unlikely she's our killer. The calmer she is, the more we can get out of her.'

'Yes, sir. This way,' said Hope.

The pair walked through a wooden door and into another room that was gloriously white. Macleod wondered if at some point Forrest Mackenzie had thought about sprucing up the offices and also giving them a colour that wouldn't mark excessively with the first year. There was little doubt to him that in twelve months' time, the place would look shabby.

'Annie Gilmartin, my name's Detective Inspector Macleod. This is Detective Sergeant McGrath. We're just going to ask you a few questions about what's happened today. Just be aware we're not seeing you as being part of this in any way. We just want to get some information about what you found, and also your impressions of your former employer.'

Macleod stared across at the woman still sitting in what would have been called a pinny. It was pink and white, flowery in design. It reminded Macleod of the seventies, a time of life that he particularly thought had got out of control. The designs have always looked somewhat crazy. Flare trousers, the white collars, the kipper ties, and ridiculous pinnies like this. They'd seemed to stay though, while everything else faded away, only to come back again. Macleod had always trusted trousers, shirt, tie and in honesty, anytime he strayed away from it, things

23

had never been good. The socks with the sandals on a beach in Spain, a particular regret.

'Annie, if you can, just run us through what happened this morning, in your own time,' said Hope.

The woman coughed. Macleod looked at the tall, thin, blonde woman beside her. It must've been Samantha and she had one arm on Annie's shoulder, the other one holding one of her hands. Annie was leaning into her, tears in the woman's eyes.

'I got the bus up and well, I came in and went to the side door, because that's what I do. There was only one car in the car park, so that was fine. I thought that's probably Mr. Mackenzie. He sometimes comes in early. These businesspeople, they do that, don't they? They just turn up when they need to be. It's not a problem. I was coming in to do the clear up from yesterday. I expected it to be just me, really, but he was here, so that was fine. I opened the door at the side, came in, got my stuff. I entered the main hall, and I didn't, I didn't see, okay? I really didn't see. I had shouted for him. That's right. I had shouted for him, but he didn't answer.'

'Where did you shout for him?' asked Macleod.

'When I came in through the small door, I shouted and I got no answer. I got my mop, and I got my bucket because I wanted to do those steps, the stoneware at the front, through the main front doors. I went up, and I entered the hall and I didn't look back at the podium. I wasn't looking that way. I was looking at the side. They've got those photographs. Big, big, big photographs of the guys doing the auction, and the women. That was quite something. I loved those. They're brilliant, but then that meant I got to the steps, opened the doors and then the doors into the steps. All the stone on the floor, I cleaned it. Went through from one to the other. I had to open the outside

24

doors, but that was the surprise.'

'Surprise?' said Hope. 'In what way?'

'Well, I put the key in to open the outside doors and they were open. The key wouldn't turn in the lock, so I pulled the handle and the door was already open. I swung them open. I cleaned it, then came back out from that area into the main hall, turned around and I saw somebody up on the podium and I thought, "Oh, Mr. Mackenzie's had a bit much. Looks like he's probably drunk."'

'Did you know him to be drunk?' asked Macleod.

'I couldn't say. I've only worked for a week. He's never been drunk in a week, but the man's been so busy running around, organizing this. You can imagine these things don't just happen overnight. I've been cleaning a lot. I did a lot of overtime, not last night, but the night before. He kindly invited me along to the auction, which was good. Then I turned, I saw him up there, and I thought he's drunk, let's go and help. I walked down, got closer and I thought that he didn't look very good and I came behind him and that's when I saw . . . well, yes, that's when I—'

'It's okay, Annie. They know what you saw,' said Samantha. 'That's right, Inspectors, isn't it? You know what she saw?'

'I've seen it, too, Annie,' said Macleod. 'I just need you to confirm to me, you took a gavel out of his head, is that correct?'

The woman started to cry and Samantha held her close.

'Sorry, Annie, I need to understand this. You took it out of his head and then what?'

'I fell down, Inspector. I couldn't, I just couldn't handle it. Did you see it? Did you see the blood?'

Macleod had seen the blood and it wasn't a lot to him, but the woman, maybe not having seen so many crime scenes, would be greatly affected. Macleod thought about certain scenes of crime he'd come into and the amount of blood lying around, an amount that made this particular murder seem like some sterilized movie, suitable to show your children.

'When you took the gavel,' asked Macleod, 'what happened?'

'I fell. I fell backwards. I hit the ground and I dropped the gavel and I looked at him and you know, he wasn't going anywhere, so I called in. I went to the office phone and I dialled 999 and I said to them, he's dead and then you came.'

'Did you notice anyone about at all?' asked Hope. 'Or any indications that anyone had been here?'

'I only—I mean the chairs were all a mess but that was from yesterday. It didn't look any different, particularly to when we left yesterday. There were still people here when I caught the bus but I mean, it was a bit of a mess. It was a big celebration with different people. I don't know.'

'You said the auction went well?' asked Macleod. 'Did you mean that in a financial sense?'

'It just looked like a really good day, Inspector. I don't know what money he made. I don't know what these things cost. I have no idea about these items. I wasn't allowed to touch them or clean them. I just cleaned the toilets and floors and everywhere else. Mr. Mackenzie would have handled the actual items.'

'Did he pay any specific attention to any in particular?' said Hope.

'Not that I could see,' said the woman, leaning in tighter to her partner.

'How long have you known him?' asked Macleod.

'I got hired for this job three weeks ago, started it less than a week ago. I barely knew the man. He seemed nice enough. Told me that as long as I did my work, he didn't care what my past was, so he obviously knew. I guess it's not that difficult to tell, is it?'

'How do you mean?' asked Macleod.

'Well, I'd have to roll my sleeves up for this job.'

Macleod understood now the marks would be there of Annie's addiction.

'And the other people that work here, Annie, how many are there?'

'I've only seen about three regulars or three I would say are office staff, the others aren't but I don't know what they had to do with anything. One of them does the publicity—she's a young girl. Another does accounts, I believe, only just started and the third one, he was some sort of security, sort of there on the day organizing everyone into the building. I don't think he knew anything about the artwork.'

'Do any of these people have any reason to be antagonistic towards Mr. Mackenzie?' asked Macleod, 'Did you ever see him having any fracas or a cross word with any of them?'

'No,' said Annie. 'We'd barely started, we didn't have time to get a cross word with anyone. We were just busy getting on, getting everything ready. It's a small team of us.'

Hope then asked a few more questions about Annie's background and about when she'd been recruited and how, but everything seemed normal and after another five minutes, Macleod asked that the woman be taken home by Samantha.

'She's clearly had a shock; keep her safe. Don't come in tomorrow, Annie, or the day after. Let our people sort this all out, and then after that you need to see who takes over and runs the company. But stay away for the next couple of days until we're clear from here. We may need to phone you so don't go anywhere.' With that, Annie was gone. Macleod sat in the makeshift interview room with Hope staring at him.

'You know we're out of our depth in this. I haven't got a clue where to start with this antique stuff.'

'No, neither do I,' said Macleod, 'that's why I've sent for a little help.'

'A little help?'

There was a knock at the door. Macleod announced that the person could come in and Ross entered with a smile on his face.

'I did what you asked, sir, and it turns out that since we blew her cover in the last case, she hasn't got anything she needs to be doing. In fact, she said it's been ridiculously quiet. They said they'll send the paperwork over but she's more than happy to give her hand.'

'When's she coming, Ross?'

'She said imminently, but I think she was at least in Inverness, if not further.'

'Okay,' said Macleod and Ross left his seniors alone.

'Who's coming'? asked Hope.

'Sergeant Clarissa Urquhart, Hope. Worked with Ross last time? He's recommended her very highly.'

'You want me to take her under my wing then?' asked Hope, 'after all, this is a murder investigation. She's only looking at part of this for us.'

'No,' said Macleod. 'As I see it, there's two strains to this. We can follow the person back. That's for you and Ross. It's what you're good at. Give me a history of this guy. Get me contacts for him and we push back through that until we find someone that wants to put a gavel in his head.'

'What will you do, sir?' asked Hope.

'I shall take Sergeant Urquhart under my wing and she's going to teach me all she knows about antiques. It's a possibility somebody did this to him because of what happened yesterday, and Urquhart is going to teach me how to work out what that is.'

Chapter 04

Macleod had been summoned to the car park of the auction house, where the uniformed sergeant he had spoken to when he first arrived was standing with Jona Nakamura. On the ground was a brochure with a ringed item on it, and the word "Ours" beside it.

'What do you make of it, Jona?' asked Macleod.

'I don't make anything of it,' she said. 'All I can see is that somebody's dumped a brochure. They've written the word 'Ours' and ringed this item. I mean, look at it. It's a stick. It's like some fancy, old walking stick.

'What's it labelled as though, Sergeant?'

The uniformed sergeant bent down and looked closely. 'It's described as an old-style walking aid,' he said. 'Oh, it's got some ornate stones in it as well. That's a bit different. Isn't it? It says it is probably going to go for anything from £50 to £100.'

'Bit expensive for a stick, for me. Is that normal?' asked Macleod of Jona.

'I don't know. I mean, I can tell you it's a stick. It doesn't look like something you'd be able to support a lot of weight on. Looks too ornate for that.'

'I was kind of hoping somebody might be able to give me a

clue if this is just a thrown-away piece of paper, or if it actually means something,' said Macleod. As he spoke, he could hear a loud car engine and the sudden squealing of brakes. Then the engine accelerated again, and he saw a small vehicle entering. It had no hood, and inside was a woman, scarf bellowing from her neck and with purple hair on top. The car pulled up in a blaze of dust, and the woman stepped out to be confronted by two police officers. Macleod watched with interest, shaking his head, before turning back to the brochure on the floor.

'You've pulled me out here to say this is evidence, but we have no idea if it's been signed by anybody of importance. It says, "Ours" on it, and it basically has ringed this item that we think is an ornate walking stick. I mean, we've got nothing here, have we?' said Macleod. 'At least nothing I can trace.'

'If you'll forgive me, Inspector, I think you've got something.'

Macleod turned around, saw the broad smile and purple hair of an upright, finely-dressed woman.

'And just who are you?' asked Macleod. 'Why is this woman here? What are your officers doing?' he said to the sergeant.

'They're doing their job, Inspector. Sergeant Clarissa Urquhart, and that piece of paper down in front of you is most certainly evidence. The fact that it says "Ours", I grant, could mean it could be anyone just having a liking to the item, but that item is not a walking stick.'

'Oh,' said Macleod. 'Well, welcome, Sergeant. Thank you for coming so promptly, but it's usually better to introduce yourself in a more formal fashion.'

The woman was wearing a smart pair of red trousers with long boots, while on top, a leather jacket with a red scarf complimented the trousers. Macleod placed her possibly into her fifties, but he was not going to be so rude as to ask.

'Well, I brought you here for this reason,' said Macleod, 'so what is it then?'

'I'm not one hundred percent sure, possibly ninety percent. I'll need to take a better look at it. And if the item is still here, even better, but I have a feeling it might not be.'

'Don't be so cryptic,' said Macleod, 'what is it I'm looking at, ninety percent or not?'

'That, Inspector, is quite possibly one of the more significant finds in the last recent years. It's Aaron's Rod.'

'What?' said Macleod. 'What do you mean it's Aaron's Rod?'

'Aaron, brother of Moses, from the Bible. Do you know the story?'

Macleod could feel the blood boiling inside him. Someone actually questioned if he knew his Bible. He'd been brought up on it, fed it every Sunday and during the week as well. Could she not spot a man from Lewis?

'Of course, I know the story. When Moses went to Pharaoh to free the Israelites, Aaron went with him and spoke for him, because Moses wouldn't speak. And in a show of strength, Pharaoh's advisors threw their staffs on the ground, and they turned to snakes. But Aaron threw his on the ground, turning it to a snake, and it eats all the rest up. So, if you're trying to tell me that that's Aaron's Rod, there's no way it's Aaron's Rod. That's a farcical notion.'

'Not farcical, Inspector. It all depends on what you believe.'

'I know my Bible, and I believe in my maker, and I tell you now, that is not the Rod of Aaron, and no mumbo jumbo around is going to make me think it is.

'Maybe not, Inspector, but that is Aaron's Rod. It's been sought after, since it was found, out in Egypt, funny enough, and by a pair of brothers who didn't know what to do with it. They sold it on, or at least so the story goes. It was surfacing around the time of the Middle Ages, and then that all goes a little bit dry, but I swear, that's it.'

'Is it valuable?' asked Macleod.

'You're talking about a staff that's mentioned in the Bible. It gets thrown into the ground, produces a snake that eats all other snakes, and you're asking me, is it valuable?' Clarissa raised her eyebrows.

'But that's not it, is it?' said Macleod. 'So once again, is it valuable?'

'Value is a little bit different in the world of antiques. Value is what you're prepared to pay for something, not what something is.'

'Well, then,' said Macleod, obviously peeved, 'would somebody be prepared to pay money for this in large quantities?'

'Most definitely, Inspector, most definitely. Shall we take a look through the back and see if it's still there?'

'Why would it still be there?' said Macleod.' 'If somebody bought it, surely, they'd take it.'

'The order could have come in from the Internet; it could have come from someone in the room. Objects like this, especially if they're seriously priced, might not get moved straight away. You're going to have to package them up. You're going to have to think about insurance in case they get lost in transit. Some of them, like this, you certainly wouldn't put into the mail, and it might get taken away under a little escort, shall we say.'

'Well, then, lead me into the back of the building and show me it,' said Macleod. 'Do you need a picture of it?'

'No,' said Clarissa. 'Besides, that's evidence on the floor, and I'm assuming our forensic officer here is going to want to do

33

something with that. Maybe you could lift a few prints off it?'

Macleod swore he saw Jona smile. He wasn't one who liked being put in his place, and so far, this new arrival was starting to annoy him.

'Lead on,' said Macleod, 'I'm right with you.'

He watched the woman make her way to the main building and was impressed by the way she strode across. There was every confidence in her movement. And whilst she was no great beauty as the world would have seen it, the way she carried herself was certainly enticing. She had that confidence that Jane, Macleod's partner, had—happy in herself, never afraid to just call things as they were.

'Your first auction house, Inspector?'

'Indeed,' said Macleod. 'I'm afraid I'm a little out of depth with the items here. Ross said you were excellent last time, and I put a lot of faith in Ross. Don't let him down.'

'Als, Als was the best, Inspector. I've never seen somebody play such a knowledgeable arts person, when he had no idea what he was even looking at. Followed my instructions to the T. Once I've had a look at the item for them, for you, I'll go and see him. It'd be good to see the young man again.'

'Just so you know,' said Macleod, 'you'll be working with me. Ross will be working with his sergeant, Hope McGrath. She's my number two. As far as this investigation goes, she outranks you.'

'But of course, I'm here to help, Inspector, not take over, but I would like to point out that as far as knowledge about antiques goes, I'm number one. So, if I say something is valuable, or I say something is a certain item, kindly trust me. I didn't get where I am by not knowing my stuff.'

Touché, thought Macleod and followed Clarissa through the

34

main auction hall, taking a route prescribed by Jona's forensic team, before entering another hall at the rear, where a number of items were laid out.

'You can't go in there like that. You'll have to get a coverall on; we haven't finished tagging these items or checking them through,' said a young man.

'But of course,' said Clarissa. 'Where are those godforsaken paint kits?'

Macleod almost laughed. The idea that these forensics suits were something that a painter wears was something that had occurred to him before, but he never would have said it out loud in such a fashion. He watched Clarissa remove her jacket and scarf before putting on the coverall suit and pulling the hood up over her purple hair. He couldn't remember Ross mentioning the fact that that woman had purple hair. That seemed a detail that Ross would certainly have lit upon.

'If you're all suited and booted, Inspector, let's have a look. By the way, Inspector, do you watch any of those antique programmes on TV?'

'No' said Macleod. 'I have no interest at all in any of that, and why people pay such money for such junk.'

'Excellent.' said Clarissa. 'I won't have to deal with an amateur expert. I shall take it you know nothing and furnish you with the appropriate knowledge.' Macleod almost rolled his eyes as he felt the woman was making sure he understood who the expert in the room was.

She strode down past tables, with various items on them. There was furniture, cabinets, there were small pipes, little silver cases, paintings and other notable collectors' items, car number plates, old adverts, posters from a bygone age. After she had walked up and down the entire hall, Clarissa turned to

Macleod. 'Well, Inspector, I'm afraid it looks like you're going to have your work cut out.'

'And why is that?' asked Macleod.

'Because it's not here. Give me a moment.' Pulling on a pair of gloves, Clarissa made her way over to a large book.

'And what's that?' asked Macleod.

'Well, normally, all records are held on the computer, but this is a register in and out of items. It's the old style with the book, but a lot of places still do it. It's just a little bit more friendly. These are people interested in antiques; they don't exactly jump for the modern ways.

'So, it's like logging these in and logging them out?'

'Yes. Who took them, signing for them, signed you've got it. I mean an electronic signature these days works in the court of law, but these people aren't a court of law,' said Clarissa. 'These people are old-fashioned. Look down there, Inspector. Can you read that?' Clarissa's finger was pointing to what looked like a lot of squiggles to Macleod. 'That's a name, Inspector.'

'It's a name written by a doctor,' said Macleod. 'You better get me a pharmacist in here so I can understand what the heck's been written.'

'Yes, I don't think that's unintentional,' said Clarissa. 'It's the number for the Rod. I've seen it in the brochure, and it's described as a staff being taken away, a walking staff. That's Aaron's Rod, sir, and it's just disappeared out of the door.'

Chapter 05

'All set?' asked Macleod.

'Yes,' replied Hope. 'It's his diary where he's been for the last while, so it's worth checking out. Obviously, if he was somewhere on the quiet, he may not have written it down, but I'll do the legwork.'

Hope had discovered the diary of Forrest Mackenzie in the drawer in his office and having glanced through the last couple of weeks, she found a number of local sites. Macleod hoped to back this up with visuals of who had visited the previous day on the CCTV that was installed in the building but having gone through the system once the day staff had arrived, he found that all data had been erased. Whoever had killed Forrest Mackenzie had done a thorough job. Jona Nakamura, the chief forensic investigator, had also come up with very little other than the man had been killed elsewhere. It made sense that the tapes had then been wiped. For they would have had to bring him in, position him on the podium and then disappear. Why would you leave a record of your height and physique readily available for any of the police to find?

'How far are you going to have to head out?' asked Macleod.

'Looking at it, most of the places are within twenty to thirty miles, so I think I could probably get most of them done by nightfall. I've told Ross to stay and get on with trolling through any contacts of Forrest Mackenzie on the internet. We'll see about purchases and that and if he can total up what was bought yesterday and who it went to. He was trying to find the purchase record of that Aaron's Rod, but I think he's finding it difficult at the moment. It appears that all the sales records have been tampered with as well. We may be able to get a trace with online activity, but he's not convinced it's going to give us the name of any buyer, if indeed they were who they say they were.'

Macleod looked around him and the day was far from over. Now into the middle of the afternoon, he was feeling sluggish, but he knew he and Clarissa had a long haul ahead. He needed to understand the history of this item. Splitting the team up had been a good idea.

'Okay, Sergeant, time to go to work. Check in with me, Hope, especially if you find anything.'

'Of course, I will, and you be gentle on her, although Ross says she can handle herself.'

'She's certainly no Kirsten, I'll give you that,' said Macleod. 'I don't think Kirsten would ever have worn such bright colours.'

'She'll blend in well with you then,' said Hope. 'I think you'd look fetching with a little red scarf on your neck.'

Macleod stared at the sergeant, not giving her the pleasure of a smile until she'd got into the car and driven off. Once she had disappeared, he turned and made his way back inside the building, ready to see what his new recruit could dig out from the auction house.

Hope spent the afternoon and well into the night, completing a circuitous route with Invershin at the centre of it. The roads were single carriage way for large parts of the drive and often she was going to places that were down little tracks to small villages, just off the main tourist routes. It was dark by the time she reached the hotel that was last on her list and only two miles north of Invershin.

Sitting back from the main road, the hotel was surrounded by trees and sat low down, so that as you approached it you got a view of its roof, and Hope could see the many air conditioners sitting on top. Or maybe they were just the outsourced heating pumps? Hope struggled to know these days. She always found it bizarre that somewhere in Scotland required air conditioning but then again it did work both ways, didn't it? Or was it the new environmental methods that were being used now? Whatever it was, there was a lot of fans in white boxes on the roof. She turned the car down the small winding hill that passed the fading sign for the McDuff hotel.

The diary said that Forrest Mackenzie had had a meet here with two people, indicated in the diary as being buyers and nothing else. This seemed strange to Hope because everyone else he had met had a name. Only these two did not. The meeting also took place at nine o'clock at night, well beyond the working day but Hope wasn't sure how the art world worked. Maybe it was over dinner, maybe it was a chat about something, or maybe it was all done socially. Being unsure, she was giving them the benefit of the doubt at the moment until she could establish further who these people were.

The front desk of this small hotel was a classical old wooden bar and behind it sat a traditional key rack. A man stood up and Hope could just see the tartan of the man's kilt over the top of the bar. He was at least six-foot-tall, a strapping man with black hair but a big broad smile.

'Good evening, are you looking a room for the night?'

39

'Unfortunately, not. I'm Detective Sergeant Hope McGrath and I wondered if you could assist me, sir.'

The man's smile faded slightly. 'Is this about the guy in the bar the other night?'

'What man in the bar?' asked Hope.

'All right, there was a bit of a fracas and one of the guests complained, I thought they might have taken it to you.'

'Was it serious?'

'No, it wasn't,' said the man, 'or at least I didn't think it serious enough to call you. But the American gentleman was rather upset.'

'Right,' said Hope and pulled their photograph from inside her pocket. 'It didn't happen to involve this man, did it?' She placed the photograph of Forrest Mackenzie on the table, a copy taken from a photograph in his own office.

'No,' said the man. 'It didn't involve him at all. He was here on a different night. Maybe two, three nights ago . . . no, five.'

Hope tallied it up with the diary and the man was correct.

'Do you remember much about his visit?' asked Hope.

'Not really. I don't serve in the bar, and I don't serve in the restaurant. I think he was here for a meal. I remember the booking. Just give me a second. From beneath the bar top, he pulled out what appeared to be a red ledger, and looked through the pages before stopping at a particular page. Hope watched the man's finger trail down the page. 'Forrest Mackenzie, that him?'

'That is indeed him, sir. What do you remember about him?'

'His face, that there, that's about it.'

'Do you know if he paid the bill?'

'Well, he must have done,' said the man, fiddling with his ear, 'I would remember if he hadn't.'

'Sorry,' said Hope, 'I meant, do you remember how he paid the bill?'

'Ugh, no, I wouldn't,' said the man. 'Morag might though, she's the missus. She runs in there. I'll get her for you.' The man turned and pointed himself towards the restaurant. 'Morag,' he shouted loudly, and Hope wondered why he didn't actually simply walk off and get her from the restaurant himself. 'Morag, woman, police are here to see you,' Hope almost laughed at the man, but he clearly couldn't see the joke of it all.

After shouting for his wife several times, he put both hands on the reception desk and stared at Hope. She was aware of him scanning her, not impolitely, and he certainly wasn't leering, but she was certainly aware she was being assessed. Whether it was the competent detective or her as a female the man liked, she was unsure.

Morag walked out of the restaurant doors and over to Hope and Sergeant McGrath began to realize why the man had stared at her. The woman opposite her had a white apron on, was dressed in a set of black trousers and a white blouse, but that was where the differences ended. She was a good six feet tall with a long run of red hair down her back tied up in a ponytail, possibly because she was working in the kitchen. Her face was taut over her cheekbones similar to Hope, but she missed the deep scar that ran down the side of Hope's face. Otherwise, one might have thought they were sisters if you didn't look too closely.

'Morag, this is Sergeant . . . Sergeant who?'

'Sergeant McGrath, ma'am,' said Hope. 'I'm sorry to bother you. There was a Forrest Mackenzie here from five days ago with a couple of other people. We're trying to trace his movements, and your husband here said that you could

41

probably help with working out how he paid and things like that?'

'Douglas said that, did he? He's bone idle and useless; follow me.' The woman spun on her heel and made for the kitchen causing Hope to almost chase after her. 'Don't worry about him on the desk, bone idle, this place would be in the ground if it weren't for me. His mother used to run it well, ran it all her life, but him, well, the only thing he can sort out is the inside of a whiskey bottle.'

Hope thought she should comment but then decided against it, letting the remark just sit. She was here for information, not to get a rundown on how the hotel operated.

'Do you remember Forrest Mackenzie?' asked Hope, handing over the photo of him to Morag as they strolled through the restaurant. There were a few diners in, and Hope was taken across the dining room to a bureau on the side, where a number of books were pulled out, as well as a laptop which was subsequently opened.

'I do remember him, though not greatly,' said Morag. 'But I do remember him coming in. He met with two people, a man, and woman. They had dinner, then entered the bar to have drinks; all seemed very amicable.'

'You didn't happen to overhear anything that they were talking about, did you?'

Morag raised an eyebrow. 'I'm not in the habit of snooping on my customers; they come for food, you understand that. Food and some drink, and company of each other. I might give them a bit of a wise crack, the odd joke but I'm not here leering over them. I don't eavesdrop.'

'I accept that quite happily,' said Hope, 'but I was just wondering if you might have caught the odd thing on the wind.'

'Well, now you come to mention it,' said Morag, 'the thing is that they were actually discussing an object. I think the man is in the antiques trade. He's got that place just down Invershin, hasn't he? Opened up a couple of days ago.' For someone who was protesting her innocence about eavesdropping on her customers, she certainly knew who they were.

'That's right,' said Hope, 'and we're just trying to track his movements.'

'Why?' asked Morag, 'Has he gone missing?'

'No,' said Hope. 'He's very much not going anywhere. The other two people, do you remember who they were?'

'No, don't think so, said Morag. 'She was a looker, I remember that. Woman like yourself, you know? Someone the men would like but business-like with it. Not some sort of floozy or anything, I don't mean that, but I mean someone who knew what they wanted. Came in to get it done, bit of class about them, but quite happy to take the look of a man, you know. You have to watch Douglas, you see, he can take a look like that. Back in the day he would have done more than look, he was quite handy but he's felt my wrath enough to stop from doing that anymore.'

Hope felt the man didn't look like he could do anything anymore, but reckoned Morag was a bit of a woman herself. 'You didn't happen to get any names?'

'The woman was Ally, they kept saying Ally, I never did get a full name, and the man was Yon or Jon or something like that.'

'Would you be able to give me a description of them?'

'I could do better than that, we do have CCTV here, just the one camera where you come in at the entrance. I like to make sure we get a photograph of anyone just in case there's a bit of trouble. It's good for the police, you know. In case you don't get

43

names or that. Just give me a minute and I'll take you through to it.'

Hope watched Morag disappear into the kitchen, then a young girl came out, presumably to stand in the dining room, ready to deal with any customers.

'I'm sorry to take you away from your work,' said Hope.

'It's fine, I'm just about over for the night. I'm just leaving Daisy there in case anybody needs an extra drink. Nice girl, polite, a bit thick really, but honest and hard-working and I'll take that any day.'

Hope wondered how Macleod was viewing their new member of the team.' Macleod valued hard work and honesty but he also expected you to come up with things every now and again, a little spark of inspiration. Certainly, Ross spoke highly of her, and he didn't speak highly too quickly. Politely, yes. He was polite about everyone, but highly was only used for those he genuinely believed were good.

Hope was led through to a back room and was plonked into a seat in front of a computer screen. She was quite amazed at the dexterity of the woman with the system, and soon, she was viewing the front entrance from just above the desk. She watched as Mackenzie entered and seemed to stand around waiting for someone else. Douglas was seen speaking to him several times before a man and a woman walked in to join him. They were on camera for barely three seconds, and they didn't look up for more than a second, catching a glimpse of the camera, and moving on quickly.

'I can move it back and forward, track it this way and that,' said Morag. 'Incredible what you can do with these new-fangled things, isn't it? I think I'll also send it to you, the image, I mean.'

44

'Perfect,' said Hope, and watched as Morag delicately adjusted the screen until it had the woman and the man looking up almost simultaneously at the single-camera.

'That one?'

'That's perfect, Morag. Thank you. If you send it to me, I can get it out to everyone. You've been a massive help. Do you remember who paid for the bill?'

'Aye,' said Morag, pressing some more buttons, and typing in a quick address as she glanced at Hope's phone. 'So that's the one you want me to use,' said Morag. 'Send it there?'

'Please,' said Hope. 'So, he paid for the bill.'

'It was the man, but it was cash.' said Morag.

'You wouldn't still have the money?'

'No. It's in the bank. I'm sorry,' said Morag. 'If I had known, I could have kept it for you.'

'No, that's fine,' said Hope. Hearing a small ping on her phone, she looked down to see an email having arrived. 'This is perfect. I can get this round everyone, and we can start looking for this couple.'

'So, this Forrest Mackenzie, is he okay?' asked Morag. 'The thing is, he seemed quite impressed with the place. I was kind of hoping he might make a more regular habit of coming here, especially with having opened his auction house down the road.'

'I bet you won't see Mr. Mackenzie,' said Hope, 'and if you do, I think you'll run a mile. Unfortunately, he is now deceased, and this is the cause of our investigations.'

'Right. Do you think these two did it?'

'Routine inquiries at this moment, Morag, and I'll thank you to keep it that way.'

'Understood,' said Morag with a touch of disappointment in

her speech. 'If they come back, I'll let you know,' she said.

'Please do.' said Hope, handing over a card before making her way out of the small hotel back into the car. She sent an email by her mobile phone to Macleod, and then followed it up with a call, too.

'Did you get anywhere?' Macleod asked.

Not even a courteous hello. 'It's been a good afternoon then, I take it.'

'Next time somebody dies, it better be away from any auction houses. I'm sick to the back teeth of the mumbo jumbo around this nonsense.'

'What do you mean?' asked Hope.

'It doesn't matter. You reckon these two are potentials?'

'Got nothing on them. Only thing was that when they came into the hotel, they checked the camera like they didn't want to be on it. Outside of that, they talked about artwork stuff cautiously. So yes, potential suspects but not even simmering yet, heating up.'

'Well, get your backside back here. You can spend the next hour learning all about the joys of Aaron's Rod because my history class is now complete.'

Chapter 06

After Macleod had waved Hope on her way on her tour of the places in Forrest Mackenzie's diary, he made his way back inside to meet up with his art world expert, Clarissa Urquhart. He found her standing beside a table with pictures of Aaron's Rod sitting beneath her. Jona Nakamura was on the other side, delicately handling the images, sifting through them. Macleod was aware that Clarissa was wearing the same white gloves that Jona had on.

'It's quite a remarkable piece, don't you think, Inspector?'

Macleod looked at the pictures of the stick. There were a couple of jewels towards the top, but they weren't gleaming like something out of a magazine cover. Rather, they were quite dull. The wood itself looked somewhat tarnished.

'It looks to me like somebody hasn't taken care of it,' said Macleod.

'No, no,' said Clarissa. 'You're wrong with that. This has been well handled. Look, there's not many scratches on it. Certainly not for the age of it.'

'What age would you say it is?' asked Macleod, 'because you're not trying to tell me that this is the same rod that Aaron handled in the Bible.'

'How old is the Bible?' asked Clarissa. 'You're heading into a world of myth and legend.'

Macleod's face suddenly became like thunder. 'You should be careful how you speak of the word of God,' said Macleod. 'You can have your own beliefs, but others are a little bit more cautious and reverent about how we speak of His Word.'

'I'm not sure that's what Clarissa meant,' said Jona. 'The Bible, the happenings in the Qur'an and other texts from back then, you could accurately describe them as myth and legend. It doesn't mean they're untrue. In Japan, we have plenty of myth and legends about how the world was made. In those days, they only knew Japan and nothing beyond it. The way they talked about it, was in that regard. The world was made. The world was Japan. Nothing more.'

'Am I to understand that you're quite a fundamental Christian?' asked Clarissa.

Macleod was quite taken aback because he didn't see himself as a fundamental Christian. By all means, he did believe in God and he did believe in a saviour, but he wouldn't have said he was dogmatic. Had it been the old defences come out? Had he been offended by the word myth?

'I'm sorry if I reacted a little strongly to you,' said Macleod, 'but this item, you're not telling me it's the Rod handled by Aaron.'

'Well, that's where the myth and legend comes in, Inspector,' said Clarissa. 'If you're asking how I can date this, we could take it away and probably get it carbon-dated and it'll give us certain time. Scientifically we'll say, "This is not it," but if you think about it, if this is a Rod that turns into a snake, all standard ways of dating things go out the window, don't they? That's where the myth and legend come in. That's where this item doesn't fall under normal scientific scrutiny.'

'It still falls under normal investigative scrutiny,' said Macleod, 'in that I want to know what it is, and where it's from. If somebody has died because of this, I need to understand the item. Whatever the myth, history, religion behind it.'

'That you shall, Inspector, but you also need to understand this item from the perspective of the people who are going for it, not just from a cold, clinical, scientific view of it. Jona will probably tell you that this stick may date back to somewhere in the Middle Ages, and she'd be right in saying that, but this stick dates back further than that, in the minds of the people who seek it.'

'When I brought you onto the team, Sergeant, I was looking for a little bit of detail about the history around this. I wasn't looking for some fantastical effort, an idea of dreams and visions that people have.'

'That's where you have to understand it, Inspector. You need to understand that these people see that Rod as the stick from the Middle Ages very possibly. That's when it appeared, and the legend of Aaron's Rod was being banged around. Now, there were stories before that, but they are so long in the past, there's no way we could ever authenticate them. Even the stories in the Middle Ages are hard to verify. The legend builds, but what really builds is the idea that this is powerful.'

Macleod raised his hand to his forehead and began to rub it. Kirsten Stewart talked in numbers and figures. She was deep in the sense that she dug and found things. This woman seemed to be erring into fantasy.

'Who's after it and why?' asked Macleod. 'Just stick with that.'

'Well, the why's quite obvious. Imagine a stick that you throw

49

in the ground, turns into a snake, and eats up all the other snakes. It's God in wood. It's got God in it. It's like the chalice, the cup of Christ. It's like the Ark. It's like anything from those times that was being touched by God and used against other people. Why are people after it? They're after it because of the power.'

'People seriously believe that sort of thing?'

'Of course, they do,' said Clarissa. 'Have you ever watched any of the antique programmes? Where they come on, people put the items in front of the experts and they say, "Tell me about it." What you get at the end is a price and that's of course very vulgar. What you get before that,' said Clarissa with a deep smile on her face, 'is what it's really worth. The story. The history. Where it's been. What part it played in the life of this world and for us. Is it a staff'? Yes, it is. But what's the point of it if it was just the staff that an old man walked with. This was Aaron's Rod.'

'Look at the jewels in it,' said Macleod. 'How is that Aaron's Rod?'

'If we look at it, they've been added after. There's an extra piece on the top. That can be interpreted two ways,' said Clarissa. It could be that somebody found an old stick and needed to dress it up a bit, to make the story, or it could be something being put on top out of reverence for what it actually is.'

'So, someone had to increase what God had already done with it,' said Macleod bitterly.

'Sure,' said Jona. 'Clarissa's not trying to argue with you. She's trying to come at a side of it to help you see what these people see.'

'Who runs around at night looking for a magic sword?' asked

Macleod. 'This is crazy.'

'It may be,' said Jona. 'But people have chased these things in history, and in recent history.'

'Who?'

'Well,' said Clarissa, 'Hitler did. He saw great stock in mystical things. You know he sought the ark, he sought the cup. He sought so much. Things that will give you power. He was deep into his mythology. The stories, they build up dreams and visions within people. They make these items worth more than what someone like me would think.'

'Forgive me,' said Macleod, 'but I was brought up with the power that comes from God and that it was all for a time long ago. The prophets, the miracles, the things that He did, were from a time in the past. It doesn't fit in the world today.'

'She's not saying it does,' said Jona.

'Okay,' said Macleod. 'Okay, so who goes after something like this?'

'Well, you've run across someone who went for it before. Lord Argyle. He had those pictures at your last case I helped you with which he stole. Lord Argyle's heavily into these sorts of things. He wants a different land. You're talking about idealists and dreamers, people who just don't want a simple fairness in the land. They want to bring about a certain type of kingdom. That's why Hitler was into it. They almost feel that they're righteous in what they do. You're talking about people who have some sort of attachment to God.'

'God, the devil, whoever,' said Clarissa. 'Whoever fits the story. The story of this one is of a power that dominates the other powers in the land. Lord Argyle fits that profile. He thinks Scotland should be different. He wanted it to be independent. He also has a deep hatred of the new order coming through. In his own way, he believes in a White race or certainly a race of people bred to control the world, in his mind, for him to control Scotland.'

'Anybody else though?'

'Well, societies that will look to protect something like this, to look after religious objects. There are others who would like to drive it on. I'll need to do some digging up for you to find out who exactly. You've also got to have something else in mind.'

'Go on,' said Macleod.

'Well, imagine if you've got all these societies who want it for its power, you're also going to have a lot of people who realize that they'll pay very well for it. This is probably something you're going to be more akin with, Inspector. People who will use it for the money they can extort with it. They'll charge over the odds for it. These fundamentalists will pay anything for it as well.'

'Okay, so you're telling me I've got nutters after it. I've got basic ordinary con men after it. Anyone else?'

'Oh, there'll be people who want to put it in the museum. People like me, except there are people like me who don't work with the law. You'll also have private collectors, people who'd pay anything for it, pay people to get it. Not because they believe in it, but because it is what it is. It's an item of note. What I don't understand is if you look at it, we've got the jewels around it, which I think are part of it. Look at the wood. It doesn't run clean through, does it? Jona,' said Clarissa, 'I want you to scan down it. My eyes are not always sharp.'

Jona looked up at Clarissa. 'What do you mean?'

'Some of that work there is exquisite, but it's not real. It's an incredible effort to cover this up.'

'What do you mean cover it up? You identified it straight

away,' said Macleod.

'If you know your stuff, you would do, but most people wouldn't know their stuff. The height's correct. That's where they made the mistake. They should have added to it. Should have made it bigger. There's a text in the Middle Ages that quotes the height of that stick, five and a half feet in common terms. The item in the picture is five and a half feet. It was probably five feet before they added the jewels. That ties in with an earlier record. If you look at the lines of the wood in places, I'm not convinced. You see that the line of the wood should change as you go down. That runs straight. Most people would turn around and say that's a copy. If you look very, very closely, I don't think some of that is wood. You have to see this item with age.'

'What do you mean?' asked Macleod.

'When you get a religious item, you want it to look magnificent but it wouldn't be. It would be old. Something can be old and powerful. It doesn't have to look pristine; why should it? What do you think, Jona?'

Macleod stood and watched Jona examine the pictures again. At five feet, she was dwarfed by Clarissa but the Asian woman stood with a pride that seemed to defy anyone larger than she.

'She's correct,' said Jona. 'Somebody added covering to this. It's like a plaster, possibly. It's incredibly well designed, like something in a movie. You know where they make the models? I can't tell exactly what it is but I can see real wood in areas that it has broken off, but underneath, it is the real wood.'

'Maybe you can get better analysis from the photographs back at the lab,' suggested Macleod.'

'I'll do that, then I'll come back to you tonight, Inspector, with more about it. I need to organize the body getting moved as

53

well, so if the two of you will excuse me, I've got a bit of work to do.' Macleod nodded and watched Clarissa and Jona gather the pictures. When they were complete, Macleod asked Clarissa to step outside. The day was overcast but at least it wasn't raining. Macleod sat down on the bonnet of Ross's car. Before him, the purple-haired Clarissa stood like she was expecting an attack. The red scarf was still around her neck, highlighting the red trousers. She looked like someone off the telly who should be into antiques.

'I just wanted to say sorry for snapping in there.'

Clarissa raised her eyebrow. 'You don't have to apologize to me, Inspector. It's quite a lot for you to take on, isn't it?'

'I work generally amongst people who kill for reasons, and you were giving me a reason. Maybe it's the fact that it's a holy item gets to me.'

'You think it could be something of God?' asked Clarissa.

'No,' said Macleod. 'I come from a Presbyterian background and all that stuff was frowned upon. It was all for yesteryear. Probably too catholic to be in the now. They do all their relics, don't they?'

'They do but understand this. I'm an art expert. I deal with the history of things. What things are to people, what makes them that, as items. They're just items. That's true of anything. We're just people but quite often we have a fiction around us. I believe that you can understand.'

'Indeed, I do,' said Macleod. 'I understand that perfectly well.'

'But treat this item the same. Don't believe the hype but understand what it does. If it is what it is, fine. But finding it, finding who wants it, who'll kill for it, doesn't mean we have to believe what it does. We just have to be aware of what that does to the minds of people.'

'I think you're going to have to present things a bit differently to me than what you're used to,' said Macleod. 'I was used to a younger woman who was able to lay things down very straight. She could look through anything, pick out the relevant detail for me. I have a feeling you might come at things from a slightly different angle.'

'I'm an old girl, Inspector. I've been round the block. Yes, I'll move to you but you're going to have to get off your ass and move to me as well. You've got a heck of a talented woman here. You need to learn how to play along as well.'

Chapter 07

Hope had endured a rather terse debriefing when she got back that night to the station. Invershin only being an hour away to the north, Macleod had allowed everyone to come back and work from the station rather than live out of a hotel further north. Jona wasn't sure just how much more she could get out of the crime scene and so most of her forensic unit had returned to the station as well. At the debrief at about 01:00 a.m., Hope had heard Jona detail how Forrest Mackenzie had the back of his skull caved in with a large blunt weapon, quite possibly a sledgehammer.

He had been picked up and placed on that podium, and a gavel put in his head, but the man had been dead prior to being positioned. Clearly, he hadn't been dead that long, for to put his arms into such a position without breaking them would have been impossible. It was three in the morning when Hope departed the station, leaving the night shift of constables and a uniform sergeant to look through various photofits of hotel people and try to make a match on the couple.

As she stood in the car park about to get into her car, Hope thought of driving to the other side of town, dumping herself on the doorstep of her new boyfriend. He had to be up in the morning, she knew that. A car hire salesman, he had his boss arriving that morning. As much as she wanted to go over there and keep him awake most of the night, Hope headed back to her own accommodation knowing it would be empty as Jona was continuing her work at the station.

When she got back to her own bedroom, Hope stripped down, got in under the covers, and lay there. She had sensed the hostility between Macleod and Clarissa Urquhart and had wondered what had been said earlier on in the day. The woman was genuinely clever and Ross seemed to have gotten on with her swimmingly, but Hope wondered what sort of a person she was. Macleod liked to be in charge, an older man, dominant, fair but stolid. She thought back to the last case of how when she got an idea in her head of how to capture the miscreants, he'd had her run with it because he knew better, knew how to catch the real prize. He didn't turn around and say stop but rather he let her be used to create a foil for him catching the big prize and Hope was not too sure how she felt about that.

She was also aware that with Kirsten having left, she was briefly the only woman in the team, certainly at the top of the team and now someone else had arrived of the same rank. Clarissa was obviously slightly older, possibly wiser in matters of police work. The old nagging doubts were coming back. Macleod always backed her now she came to think of it. Yes, he'd supported her, but she was never entirely sure what he thought of her. Well, she was still in the team so clearly, she wasn't rubbish but Kirsten Stewart he had promoted, he had told to go. She was now with the secret services capable of operating on her own.

Hope never felt that the hand was taken off her. Even when Macleod had disappeared to go and look after his partner, he'd still come to the rescue, still made the key decisions. Hope remembered the Fort Augustus incident well and she aspired to have the focus that Macleod had.

It was half-past six when the phone rang and Hope swore at it. She threw back the covers, stood up, grabbed the phone to her ear and announced herself in an uncompromising fashion.

'What?'

'Am I speaking to Sergeant McGrath?'

'Yes, this is McGrath.'

'Sorry to bother you, Sergeant. It's Constable Hanley. You left me with photographs to go through last night. I've got a match.'

Hope was padding now into the kitchen, starting to switch on the kettle.

'What do you mean, a match?'

'A match for the photos you gave me. You gave me a photo of a man and a woman and you said match them up. See what we've got on the database. Well, I found her.'

Hope stopped, flicked off the switch of the kettle. 'You found her? Who?'

'Allison, Allison Danvers. We've got an address, too.'

'Right,' said Hope, suddenly coming alive. 'Get hold of uniform, tell the desk sergeant I need at least five or six people. We need to go to that address. See if she's there. I'll be in, in, oh, call it forty-five minutes. Just getting changed now. Get a team of them together and ready. Good work, Emily. Oh, by the way, where's the address?'

'Inverness, Sergeant. West side of, just as you leave. Looks like a flat.'

'I'm on my way. Get them ready.' With that, Hope tore back into her bedroom, pulled open a drawer and quickly pulled on a pair of pants and a bra. Throwing on a T-shirt and jeans, she put her feet into her DM boots before grabbing her leather jacket and checking she had all her paraphernalia with her. With a last look at the mirror, she realized her hair was a complete mess. Grabbing a hair tie, she bunched it together, pulled it out the back into a ponytail, and snapped the hair tie over it. It would have to wait. She hadn't even had a shower either. She must smell like something bad.

While she was on the road to the station, Hope put a call through to Macleod. He mumbled something about her getting on to it, asked her to handle it, and he'd be there as soon as he could. On arrival at the police station, Hope found six uniformed officers ready to go. Rather than go inside, she simply drove off with them to the address they've been given. A uniformed sergeant jumped into Hope's car and she recognized the tall man from the station.

Sergeant McCrae was a reliable sort, probably assigned to this because his physical presence would have been extremely helpful. Whenever they felt they had runners, McCrae was employed because he was quick, could organize a team, but could also hold on to the wildest of them.

'We've got a car reg for her as well,' said McCrae, sliding into the passenger seat. 'But the address is maybe two months old. We're not sure she'll be there. Possibly might have moved on.'

'But she's clearly not hiding out,' said Hope. 'That's a good thing. Not some sort of hitwoman.'

'Indeed, but as far as I understood it, you only picked her up because she was at dinner with the deceased man,' said the Sergeant. He'd clearly been reading what reports had been written so far, keeping himself up to date. Always wise when you're going to apprehend a suspect that you knew roughly who they were.

The sun was well up as Hope arrived at the west side of Inverness with the roads alive, being a weekday. Parking up, she made her way quickly towards the front door and checked the names and numbers attached to various buttons which would call the individual flats. Allison Danvers' name was there and it was the top flat. Hope pressed the button for the lower floor, asked someone for a random name, got told they didn't live there. She apologized and made her way back to the car. When she got behind the driver's seat, Sergeant McCrae pointed over to a car parked outside the flats.

'That's hers. Nice little number, too, isn't it?'

Hope was not a car person, but she recognized the little two-seater sporty number and thought of driving it. *Was this person also from the art world? Did Allison Danvers play a part in what went on? Well, they would soon find out.*

'Okay. Let's go,' said Hope. 'Sergeant, you take it. I'll run cover behind here in case there's a runner.' The sergeant nodded, got out of Hope's car and waved to the rest of his team. He then approached the house. On pressing the button for the door, he got no answer from the flat and so pressed another one to be let in through the front door. Hope watched him make the way up the steps as she sat in her car, watching outside. She got several calls over the radio. McCrae had gone all the way up the steps, reached the top flat. There had been no answer at the door, and he was now trying to open it.

They'd have to be careful about breaking and entering. This woman was a suspect in a murder crime, but they didn't have the right to just simply go storming in. Hope wondered what to do. McCrae would look for any reason he had to get in there. Possible illegal activity or someone in trouble but they were on a sticky wicket if they just broke in.

All these things raced through Hope's mind but then she saw a woman walking out of the front door. She thought about Allison Danvers from the photograph on the CCTV. She had long black hair, was fairly petite. Maybe only about five foot four and she certainly cut a wave with the way she looked. The woman that had exited the building was making her way over to the sports car. Hope opened her own car door, shouting over. The call she gave was innocuous, a simple hey but she saw the woman glance at her and then run.

Hope grabbed the radio, 'We've got a runner, McCrae, downstairs. Dressed in black.' With that, Hope tucked the radio into her belt and ran after the woman. The set of flats, which was large and concrete, was on an estate that Hope would not have described as salubrious. It was considerably basic, probably inhabited by people who worked hard in factories on low paid jobs and whilst it was certainly not run down, it was definitely at the rougher end of life.

She watched the woman cut through a back alley and followed after her. Hope ignored the young boy she ran past who catcalled and yelled out 'bitch fight', instead focusing on the woman ahead. Hope could see that she had a mobile phone in her hand and was clearly talking to someone as she ran.

Hope was well built and quick but the woman was cutting in and out of back alleys that Hope didn't know and every time she got to the end of one, she'd have to take a quick look to see where the woman was. It also meant that uniform were not quite sure where to go. Hope reached the end of one of the narrow alleyways and the woman was gone. Taking a quick right, Hope ran some hundred metres, couldn't see the woman, turned around, retraced her steps, and ran a hundred metres the other way. It was then at the corner of a street, she saw the woman getting into a car.

There was a taxi sign across the top of it. 'Blast,' thought Hope, running quickly to try and pick up the number plate. 625, the last three digits was all she got. She picked up the radio and called out to uniform. 'Black taxi. Number plate, 625. She's in there, McCrae. Get the cars around and try and stop her. Put it out to the rest of the force too—see if we can pick up where she's going.'

Hope began the walk back to her car because she was well aware that she couldn't chase the woman now. It would be up to uniform and their cars to see if they picked her up. Her mobile rang as she walked along. Looking at it, she saw her new partner was making a call.

'Clarissa, it's Hope.' Hope's breathing was heavy and the woman must have wondered what she was up to.

'Didn't catch you at a bad time, did I?' asked Clarissa. 'Ross said you might have stayed over at your man's.'

'I'm out on the street. We've just been chasing a suspect, the one we found at the hotel. They came up with an ID for her last night.'

'Yes, I just was doing a bit of checking,' said Clarissa. 'I have no idea who she is. She's not in the antique circles. Really have no idea why she would want the staff.'

'Well, she's whizzing around in a taxi at the moment,' said Hope. 'Maybe we'll catch up with her but thank you for that and for what it's worth, I'd rather have been at my man's house last night.' Hope switched off the phone, put it away in her pocket, and trudged wearily back to the car. Maybe uniform would grab her; maybe McCrae would come up with the goose. Once back in the car, Hope began to drive out of the estate. She got a position check on McCrae and realized that he had cleverly cordoned off the entire estate. The taxi was still in there, they would find it, but Hope was worried she'd already be gone.

As she made her way back across Inverness, a phone call came in. It was McCrae.

'Hope, we've got her, or rather we've got the taxi. It stopped off just by the bridge in town. She's not on board anymore. Said he dropped her about four or five streets away. I've had the car scanning around, but she's gone. I'm sorry. She's definitely gone.'

Hope smacked the steering wheel with her hand. It'd been so close, but the woman was clearly on the lookout for people coming for her. She hadn't been in her flat, or at least she'd gone down and hidden away while the police officers went up.

Hope thanked McCrae, and then prepared herself for the assault that would be from Macleod. The one suspect, the one link was gone, and because she'd run, she was definitely a link. What had Ali Danvers to do with this missing piece of art? It was going to be a long day. If she was quick, she might get a shower at the station before Macleod arrived.

Chapter 08

The time was eight o'clock and Clarissa Urquhart pulled up in her small two-seater sports vehicle at the rear of Inverness Police Station. She had been used to operating at a discreet distance from her Glasgow base but now that she was asked to specifically assist Macleod's team, she took the chance to bring some things over from her temporary flat and set up a desk for herself in the office of the murder investigation team. Walking through the single door into the long office, Clarissa saw one figure at the far end that she recognized.

'Goodman Alan. You're early as ever. Where do I dump my stuff?'

Alan Ross stood up, walked across, and shook hands with Clarissa. 'Welcome. Great to have you onboard for a bit. I know we had a brief introduction again yesterday but feels like you're part of the team now. Even coming for a desk, and just opposite me. That's where Kirsten used to sit.'

'Kirsten? I figured you were a team of four until quite recently. Hope nothing untoward happened to her.'

'No, no. Moved on in the world. Gone and joined other departments,' said Ross. 'Let me take that stuff for you.'

Ross took the cardboard box from Clarissa and placed it delicately in the middle of her desk. He watched as she took various artifacts from it and photographs, placing them round the desk, then he saw a pen set with a lot of gold around it.

'That must have cost a packet.'

'Not if you buy it in the right place. A lot of it is not particularly good gold.' Clarissa laughed. 'I might like the expensive stuff but I'm a policewoman. I don't earn enough to get it. I should have been a criminal.'

'The boss will be in soon. Hope's already out and about chasing down an ID on a woman she saw in the hotel last night. Might be a bit of luck. Get to the bottom of this quickly.'

'Your boss is a bit touchy when it comes to things of a religious nature, isn't he?'

'Yes. The boss had a very strict upbringing,' said Ross, 'on the Isle of Lewis. Very Presbyterian. People like me wouldn't have been in the picture but in his defence, he's never said anything to me. I know he struggled at times with my sexuality, but he's been all right and he'll be all right with you. Give him time. You're just a little bit more colourful.'

'I'm also a little bit older. Been around the block unlike the rest of you. I take it Kirsten wasn't an older girl like me?'

'No. Kirsten was the youngest in the team. Very clever, very astute. Very like him in that she was very obsessive. They'll know who's done something even before all the evidence is in. They read people. Me, I'm just your plain old workhorse.'

'Don't play yourself down, Alan. You're quite a charming guy with it.'

'Oh, here he is. Morning, boss.'

Macleod strolled into the room looked down and saw Clarissa with her cardboard box on her desk. 'Good,' he said. 'Getting yourself settled in. When you've got a moment, please come through.'

Clarissa simply turned and followed Macleod into his room where she watched him hang his coat. 'Your job today, Sergeant, is to get me the recent history of that Rod. Find out who's been interested in it. Find out why. Find me where it's gone. I take it you have the necessary contacts to look into things like that?'

'Yes,' said Clarissa. 'It won't be easy though. I may need to pop out, but I'll get to it.'

'Ross is going to have his hands full because he's going to be going through interviews of people at the auction. We've got uniform speaking to the crowd that was there, trying to take note of anything untoward. It's a thankless task and it's sifting through nothing for the one tiny detail, but it's what he's good at. We brought you in because you're good at the art stuff. Get me an answer.'

'Well, that was positively inspirational,' said Clarissa. 'I love my job and I'll do it for you, Inspector; you don't have to worry about that. I understand I look a bit different. I act a bit different. I am not in awe of you like the rest of your team, but be in no doubt I'm on top of it.'

'Glad to hear it, Clarissa. Oh, and one other thing.'

Clarissa looked up, tensing slightly. Ready for another assault on her style or manner.

'Welcome to the team. Pleasure to have you here.'

There was almost feeling in it, she thought. *It wasn't like he was doing it through gritted teeth.*

'Oh, and, Inspector, can you give me your mobile number again? Your private one.' Clarissa bent down taking off her shoe. It had a small heel and was much more stylish than the

DM boots worn by Hope. Macleod watched in fascination as the heel was twisted, removed and a small phone was taken out.

'Just a little trick I have up my sleeve. Sometimes when you go to these art dealers, they take away your mobile phones. You might want to pop to the toilet and make a call. Let people know what's happening. This is the smallest mobile phone in the world, very clever.' Macleod nodded and passed over his phone details. 'I can order one for you too, sir. Be back shortly.' With that, Clarissa left to take her position at her desk at the far end of the office.

Clarissa was aware over the next two hours that Macleod kept looking out of his office to see what she was doing. Generally, the phone was on her ear, and she was talking to various dealers around the country. Some were old friends, some were just contacts, and some she was pitching in the dark using old codes and cover names that she hadn't brought to the floor in a while. Her last cover had been blown but at least on the phone it was easier to make one up or follow an old one. You didn't have to get dressed up in a style with mannerisms that were appropriate.

Clarissa saw Hope return looking rather dejected. She and Ross were pulled in for a quick debrief before Ross returned advising that the woman who he was looking for had done a runner. Clarissa was well in the dark about the woman, something she had advised Hope of that morning. She began to sense a little tension building amongst the team.

'Things always get like this if things don't happen fast?'

'Like what?' asked Ross from the opposite desk.

'Get sort of jumpy and despondent.'

'Our boss is always despondent. He's never happy until it's done, dusted.'

'But you just keep going, don't you, Als?' Clarissa saw the smile coming back on his face.

'You don't want to be start saying Als, I'm Ross. We're out in the car, you can call me Als but in here, I'm Ross. I don't get my first name and frankly, I don't want to—this is work.'

'I know what you mean,' said Clarissa. 'I just called him sir. I can't get past all the old ways either and being back in the buildings again bring it all back. When you're out pretending to be an art dealer and that, you've got the swagger; it goes with it, darling. Can't use that sort of talk in here?'

Ross smiled. 'Are you getting anywhere though? He'll be wanting some sort of update soon; that's why he keeps looking out. He's itching you see, itching to do but you've got a bit of the work that he can't do. I go through all the boring stuff, churning out, keeping all the details going. He's in there with the brain churning around, sends Hope out to do the running around. He used to bounce everything off Kirsten because they were so alike but now, if he wants to bounce something off somebody, he hasn't got anyone, so it's going to be you. At least you're working an area he doesn't understand. You've got a bit over him on that one.'

'Well, we might be getting somewhere. At least I can give him a bit of background.'

Clarissa heard the office door of Macleod open. She saw him staring down.

'How are the interviews coming, Ross?'

'Uniform's still sending them in, sir, feeding through them at the moment. Most of it is just humdrum. Nice day out at the auction house.'

'Inspector, if it's me you want, just ask,' said Clarissa. 'I'll give you an update if you want.' Macleod looked slightly surprised, but he gave a nod and turned back into his office.

'That's a yes,' said Ross. 'Don't keep him waiting. Not good to wake the lion.'

'Strikes me more as a bear,' said Clarissa, smiling and grabbing a few papers off her desk. 'Still, he should be happy with this.' Clarissa was surprised when she found Macleod holding the door open for her. He then offered a chair at a table at the side of the office before closing the door behind her.

'This is where we generally have our chats. If you're standing before me in front of the big desk it's usually a formal reprimand,' said Macleod. Clarissa felt he was very heavy in the way he said it but then she saw him smile.

'That was a bit of a joke, wasn't it, sir.'

'You know we don't do sirs anymore. You keep calling me Inspector, that's fine if you want detachment and you're not planning to be here long, but Clarissa, we're working together and it's tough enough as it is with the way you and me are, so it's Seoras, especially when we're on our own together.'

Clarissa put her papers on the table, gave her hair a shake and smiled. 'Okay, Seoras, we got off to a bit of a rough start.'

'I'm an old boy and you said you were an old girl, so you know how it feels. This whole thing isn't right. No more airs and graces, they said. No more respect, I thought, but I'll give you the respect now. You tell me what you know about this Aaron's Rod because at the moment we're lacking any direction on where to go.

'Well, it's not been easy but I've gone round most of the dealers I know and the ones who could handle this kind of traffic. Most are not aware at all but I spoke to my contact in Dundee and Lord Argyle has been on the lookout. Of course, he doesn't do it himself—there's people associated with him.

The contact himself hasn't dealt with the item but he was asked about it. He pushed out, got some feelers. A few other people further down the chain complained. It seems there's a group after it, a strongly religious group. Not in a good way either, Seoras, if you see what I mean.'

'You mean people who would actually trust it would do things, that it actually will eat the snakes so to say?'

'Exactly. I'm trying to get a name for the group Lord Argyle's mentioned with. He's been attached before to various religious items. Not that we have that many floating about in this country, certainly not things like this. I mean Aaron's Rod, it's a once-in-a-lifetime probably, certainly for most people.'

'Anything else you can tell me about this group?'

'From what I heard they haven't got it. At the moment, all we know is that the Rod was in the building, it was sold, and it's gone. Ross hasn't found out who it actually was sold to. I don't think it's the religious group that were buying it although they were interested.'

'Do you think they were there in person?' asked Macleod.

'I doubt it, but if we had CCTV footage of the whole day, I could probably spot them.'

'You could spot them?'

'Yes. You can tell people with the way they love their art. Some people look at things as a thing of beauty, others look at it as a thing of power. The zealot, he was looking to use that power. Not all detective work is done on a computer, ticking boxes, crossing off coincidences. A lot of it is done with the eyes. A lot of it's done understanding people.'

'Preaching to the choir here,' said Macleod. 'I'll see what we can dig up then. Did you get anything else?'

'Only this religious group is ready to buy. They're happy

to move on it. If Argyle is at their head, I think we should make a move on him. Go straight after him, trap him. Set up a sting, make them think we've got it. I could use contacts to get through that way; we can learn about them then.'

'No,' said Macleod. 'I mean the idea is not a bad one but what are we doing? We're bringing in Argyle? We're finding out he's a nutter.'

'Zealot, religious zealot, vastly different to a nutter,' said Clarissa in as serious a face that she could produce.

'So, he's dangerous then.'

'Oh yes,' said Clarissa. 'You wouldn't think somebody looking for artwork could be dangerous. This guy would put a hit on someone to achieve this. He would order somebody to be killed. I've worked around him, and we've never been able to prove anything, but I've seen dealers quake when you mention his name. He's at the head of something that we've never been able to put a handle on. He moves in such high circles that you have to be concrete before you do anything. We've barely been able to mix a good mortar. So, trust me, I'd love to get hold of him.'

'No, the focus at the moment is who killed Forrest Mackenzie. We don't want to scare people off by jumping in with both feet to do something else. Danvers on the run, that's where the attention should be, but keep on at it, Clarissa; trace the Rod. If she took the Rod, it'll come out from her to sell on or she'll pass it to Lord Argyle, but from what you've said, his people don't have it. She'd have to trade if she wanted to sell. I'm guessing a sale would attract too much attention. I assume she'd be able to market this anywhere in the world.'

'Very much, but you'd have to get it out of here. People will be looking; that's if she's got it. But if she's got it, why come

71

back and kill Forrest Mackenzie? What did he know?'

Macleod stood up, turned, and looked out the large window at the back of his office. 'I don't know what it was like working on the art side, but murder investigations are never clear at the start. You sit, then you try to grab a thread and that thread falls apart, and you grab another one and it falls apart. But at some point, you pull on a good one. Either that or somebody dies and there's even more threads.' Macleod turned back and smiled at Clarissa. 'I'm rarely happy at the start of an investigation, but at the end of the last one, somebody actually described me as quite buoyant.' He gave a grin.

'I'll get back on it, Seoras. I'm probably going to head out today, go and see people in the flesh. If you need me, give me a call.'

'I will do and, Clarissa, make sure you give me the number of that, the old phone as well. I tend to ignore any number I don't recognize on my phone.'

'Will do,' said Clarissa and she stood up and extended a formal hand to Macleod. He took it and gave it a gentle shake. 'Thanks for letting me in. I don't do standing around well; it's nice to be needed. I hear I have a lot to live up to replacing your last one.'

'You're not a replacement,' said Macleod. 'I couldn't replace her, but you'll be fine. You'll be more than fine. Now, go find me that Rod.'

Chapter 09

Ross picked a way along the twisting road, his destination, Inchnadamph, a small village near Assynt. A woman had been found dead by a bed and breakfast owner out for a walk with her dog. She seemed to have collapsed, and the officers who had arrived had found a small nick around the woman's neck, causing them to deem the death as possibly suspicious. The station had been advised and as Ross was still waiting for many of the interviews to come in from the uniform, the Inspector decided to send his constable out for a quick look.

In truth, Ross was welcoming the distraction, getting a chance to drive into the late afternoon, cutting across the north of the country and to places that he rarely travelled to. Ross loved the open country. This particular road took him out amongst fields with mountains on either side, before cutting up through Ledbeg and Stronchrubie, to arrive at Inchnadamph. To the west lay Lochinver where he remembered visiting the lifeboat station there. The west of Scotland always felt so much more remote.

When you started off in the south, you had the borders, which were more like countryside. Then you had the great cities of Glasgow and Edinburgh before moving to Perth in the Highlands. Perth was like Inverness, a big city surrounded by wildness, but when you cut away over to the northwest, there were no large settlements. Everything was small. Little roads to trundle along, large lochs to look at and mountains, usually on either side. It wasn't the grandeur of the Cairngorms, but rather something different, something even wilder.

The wee villages you passed through, most did not have the big shops that the south had. A lot even had long established local shops that had not yet been taken over by today's retail tigers. It reminded Ross of a day gone by. With his sexuality, most people would have believed he preferred to be in the big city, but that was to judge a person by a name, by a given description, and not by the person himself. Ross and his partner loved this part of the world, for they adored the outdoors, to go strolling, to walk, to see all the colours and the changes through nature. It was only a pity, that at the end of this travel, he was going to end up looking at a dead body.

As Ross made his way into Inchnadamph, he realized it wouldn't take long to find his police colleagues. The place only had four or five houses. One looked like a bed and breakfast. There was a field centre, according to the signpost, and an old kirk, which was where he was making his move to. As he pulled up outside of it, he left the single-track road with its well-worn patches of tarmac covering potholes that had developed. Exiting the car and looking at the kirk, a name for an old Scottish church, there was a stone wall with moss growing on top of it.

In other places, this would be considered a tourist attraction, but Ross looked across at the graveyard around it, large coarse pieces of stone sticking out with names of people long gone.

The kirk was a white building, looking like a large hovel with one central chimney-like piece coming out of its top. There were a few trees within the churchyard, sporting green that would possibly die off in winter. Just beyond the kirk, he could see the sea, reminding him what he loved about the place. You had the mountains, the sea, everything so close together, and on a good day with a nice, fresh wind, you could smell it all.

Ross walked up alongside a police car and was greeted by a constable. 'You must be Ross. John Anderson. We're kind of a bit of long way out here. I've taken the woman inside the kirk. She'd been out for a walk with her dog and she's a wee bit freaked out, to be honest, but she's got nothing to do with it.'

'Where's the body?' asked Ross.'

'Come into the churchyard, and I'll take you and let you see.' Ross made his way through a small gate into the mowed grass of the churchyard, making his way round a small stone building. They found a large piece of slate kept up from the ground by four stone pillars. It was only about knee-high but clearly marked where someone had died, buried beneath this simple tombstone. On top of the tombstone, lay a woman face down.

'This is how you found her?' asked Ross.

'Yes,' said John. 'We barely touched her. I did take a close look. The only thing I've moved is her hair back at the side there. That's when I saw the nick and where I tried to get a pulse initially, but when I moved the hair, saw the incision, I thought the worst. She was cold to the touch as well.'

'Did the dog owner recognize her at all?'

'No. I don't think anybody around here would. We know most of the locals.'

Ross looked down, and the hair that had been moved back had seemingly fallen over again. He looked at the black jeans, black boots, and the black coat. 'What time was she found?' asked Ross.

'About lunchtime. Well, it looks like she was dead for a while.'

'When you say lunchtime, what time exactly?'

'Well, I think the lady found her about one. We got here about two, once we got the call. She panicked, cried, then had to walk back for the phone signal, to call us.'

'There's nothing else around the site here untoward, you can see?'

'No, except there's possibly car tracks, but then cars come in here all the time. Look at it. It's a little picturesque church, isn't it? Tourists love this sort of thing.'

Ross looked about. It was a delightful church, but he knelt down, taking some gloves out of his pocket. He brushed back the hair. It was dark like the woman's clothing, but when he pushed it back, he found she was pale in skin. Ross stared at the face, finding it vaguely familiar. In fairness, he was only looking at half her face. One shut eye, one side of a nose, one cheek. Something was clicking with him.

He stood up and made his way around to the side of the building. Taking out his phone, he quickly started flicking through the photographs on it until he got one that had been attached to an email message. He set the brightness on his phone to maximum and came back, kneeling down in front of the woman again. Her hair had fallen once more but Ross pushed it back and placed the mobile phone beside the woman's face.

'John,' asked Ross. 'Would you take a look here? Would you say that's the same woman?'

'Well, the photo is a bit grainy. That's CCTV I take it on the mobile phone, but I would. That's a damn good likeness. Who is she?'

'Allison Danvers. We were looking for her this morning, early. Now she's here and dead. Last seen in a taxi on the far side of Inverness.'

'It's a reasonable hike to get up here. What time was she down there?'

'Prior to half seven, possibly.'

'Well, the time frame fits. She could have got up here and been killed. She would have been cold when I touched her.'

Ross stood up, waving John over with him. 'Where did you say the woman was who found her?'

'She's currently with my colleague in the kirk. I was standing outside just to guard the scene.'

'Good,' said Ross. 'So, nobody else has been on here except you and me?'

'Yes, and my colleague, briefly, but nobody else.'

'Right, John. I want you to keep guard here. Let no one in. I need to make a call and looking at the phone, I might have to move down the road a little bit.'

'Understood but you can borrow my radio if you want. It's in the car. We get the airwave through from here. It's a bit patchy in places but it should be okay here.'

Ross made his way over to the police car, opened the door and stepped into the passenger seat. He picked up the radio, called the main station saying his call sign and asked for a patch through to Macleod.

'I've got her,' said Ross. 'I've got Hope's woman.'

'What do you mean you've got her?' said Seoras. 'You went to Inchnadamph? It's meant to be a routine job. I was expecting you back in an hour.'

That's a bit steep timewise, thought Ross. But he ignored the

77

comment. 'I've checked with the photo on my mobile phone. I believe this body is Allison Danvers.'

'She's gone from Inverness up to Inchnadamph, and she's dead?'

'From what I can see, there's a wound into the side of her neck. Not sure what that means. We'll need to get Jona up here to tell us how she died, but the scene's pretty good as there's not been many people on it. We may get something. If you get the troops running, I'll go and interview the woman who found her, see if we can find anything else.'

Ross made his way to the small kirk, and on entering, found a woman sitting on a small wooden bench with a tall constable in front of her.

'DC Ross. I'm here to have a word with our dog walker.'

'Her name is Hayley McCallister and she owns the B&B not far from here. She was just having a walk with her dog when she found our body.'

'Okay,' said Ross. 'I'll take it from here. You can pop outside if you want a quick breather.'

The constable nodded at him and made his way outside while Ross sat down beside the woman.

'Bit of a shock. Guess you don't find too many dead bodies up here. Especially not like that.'

'I don't think I've ever found anyone like that,' said the woman. 'It wasn't me that found her anyway. It was Jonzie.'

'Jonzie?' queried Ross, then realized that something was sniffing around his leg.

'My dog, Jonzie. He started pulling at her. I think he thought she was asleep. He's quite new. Likes to play with people. If you don't give him enough attention, he starts grabbing at you.'

Ross could feel something pulling his trousers. 'I see,' he

said. 'Did you see anyone else here, Hayley, when you arrived?'

'No. It was all quiet. I guess pretty much as it is out there now. We don't have much of a village here. There are a few people about, but I mean, a police car sitting outside here wouldn't even be noticed unless people drive past. It's quiet. Why on earth would somebody kill someone up here?'

'Why do you think she was killed?'

'Well, that police officer said it, didn't he? The marking on her neck and you're here. There must be something untoward if you're here.'

Logical deduction, thought Ross, *fair enough*. 'Hayley, did you see anybody unusual today? Even within the village?'

'Well, there was someone in a large Land Rover. Posh looking chap. I haven't seen him before. Don't know who he was.'

'What direction was he going?'

'He just passed the B&B; that's my B&B is just off the main road. He would have been going south to north.'

'Did you see him turn in here?'

'No,' said Hayley.

'Did you recognize anything about him? Could you give me any details about his features?'

'No,' said Hayley. 'I didn't get a good look at him.'

'But you got a good enough look at him to know he wasn't local?'

'I got a good enough look at the Land Rover to know that it wasn't a local one. I think if it was anybody around here, I would have spotted who it was in the cab, but in truth, I couldn't tell him from Adam.'

'What colour of hair did he have?' asked Ross.

'He had a hat on. One of those—is it a ghillie? Something like that.'

'You mean those tweed-looking ones for hunting and fishing?' asked Ross.

'Yes. They're not cheap, are they?'

'I wouldn't know,' said Ross. 'Never bought one, myself. Did he turn down here in towards the church?'

'I couldn't tell,' said Hayley. 'At that point, I'd turned back in a way. You don't think of it, do you? If someone strange is there, you don't think, "Oh, I better keep an eye on them in case they go murder someone."'

'It may not have been him, and she may not have been murdered,' said Ross, 'but all the same, it's not a nice thing to find. Things are going to get a bit busy up here for a while, but we might need a couple of rooms, places to stay. Are you full at the moment?'

'Not at the moment,' she said. 'I might be able to do a room or two.'

'Good,' said Ross. 'We might just need that.' Then, he felt a sharp bite in the back of his leg. 'Oh, damn well nipped me.'

'He does that. I'm not paying him enough attention, you see.' Ross began to wonder if there was another B&B in the area.

Chapter 10

The drive up to the Inchnadamph was an unsettling one for Hope, as unlike Ross, she didn't take in the surroundings in the same way. Brought up in Glasgow, she found the countryside at times rather mundane, especially when driving through it. She would have rather been scrambling across it, backpacking, setting a tent up somewhere. This sedate drive, round roads that you had to concentrate on because of their finickity little bends meant that she arrived at the small kirk slightly frustrated and feeling somewhat jaded. As she approached the small car park, Hope saw Jona Nakamura, once again ahead of the game. The large forensic van hadn't turned up yet, but Jona clearly jumped in her own car with an assistant or two, trying to get to the scene before it was spoiled. Ross was sitting on his own car bonnet and gave a smile as his boss approached.

'There's truly not a lot to see,' said Ross. 'The body is over there on the flat tombstone, beside the small building. I've sent Hayley, the first informant, back home; here's the address, but in reality, it's back down that road, take a right, take a right, take a left, bed and breakfast. There's not much she can say anyway. She did see someone passing through the town, in a

Land Rover. I was trying to see if I could see it, but in reality, we've only got a type of car and a colour, which isn't checking out. I think the first informant may not have been totally accurate with the description she gave me. Besides, we can't trace the Land Rover to here, only passing through the village with a stranger on board. There's plenty of other strangers that have passed around here, I reckon, holidaymakers. It could have been anyone.'

'It could have been, Ross, but that just isn't anyone in there, is it? You reckon that's the woman I saw?'

'Looks like she might be the one; according to the picture, I'd say she's a match, but take a look for yourself. I haven't searched the body or anything. I left that for Jona to do, but from the quick scan I took before I got out of the scene, there doesn't appear to be anything. You've got two uniformed officers here, both constables; they've just been keeping the place clear so far.'

'That's perfect, Alan, you get yourself back to Inverness. Seoras is jumping out of bed since those auction house reports are starting to come in now. He wasn't expecting you to be up here this long.'

'Well, I wasn't either,' said Ross. 'I did pick up some of the stuff on a brief mobile connection I got once I drove out of here. There's nothing like sitting at a desk and going through it. I guess he's finding it a bit strange now, Kirsten not being here.'

'The two of you did kind of change in and out of all the data collection, pulling the things together. I'm not sure our new sergeant would be so keen.'

'She's being tagged along by the boss. I think she'd be keen to do anything where he wasn't involved. They didn't seem quite a happy pair when I saw them.'

Hope laughed. 'Go on, get going, I'm going to take a walk in and see what Jona has discovered.'

Leaving Ross to depart the scene in his own car, Hope opened the small gate and made her way into the graveyard. Jona didn't turn round from where she was looking at the body, but her hand shot out, indicating that Hope should stay back. Knowing better than to step anywhere, Hope stood her ground for the next four minutes watching Jona work away with the body before the diminutive Asian woman stood up, turned around, and walked over to Hope. She pulled back the hood and smiled.

'Lovely looking church, isn't it? A very scenic place to die.'

'Is that meant to be a joke?'

'Just keeping the mood light. That's what we do in the forensic department. If you can't look at death with a smile, you don't deserve to work with me.'

'Don't let Macleod hear you say that. Unprofessional, he'd call it.'

'Sure, like he'd make me walk. I know too much about him now.'

'Is he still on the meditation sessions with you?' asked Hope. 'Is that where you've been disappearing off?'

'It's harder to keep tabs on me, isn't it, now you've got that boyfriend across town? Still, he's giving you a good boost; look at the complexion on you, girl.'

Hope blushed slightly. 'That's enough. What we got here?'

Jona grabbed some coveralls for Hope's shoes and asked her to walk with her over towards the body. One of Jona's assistants was taking photographs this way and that. When Jona received a nod from him, she reached down and turned the dead woman over.

'Certainly looks like her,' said Hope. 'Anything inside in the jacket?'

'Nothing. A little bit of cash, maybe twenty quid—that's all,' said Jona.

'Nothing to identify her.'

'Very strange. No driving license, no purse, nothing.'

'All the pockets are empty.'

'That's a bit strange, isn't it?'

'It's like somebody wanted to wear something in case they got caught. Something that wouldn't give them away. Like they knew they were being sneaky.'

'When they were in the hotel, they looked up at the camera. Not with the corner of their eye either, they looked straight at it. Took a moment of recognition, then they moved away quickly. That's not normal, Jona. Somebody who's good at this sort of thing, somebody who doesn't want to be seen, will see these things in the corner of their eye. They're looking for them before they get caught in the spotlight. We might have a couple of amateurs here.'

'Well, there was nothing amateur about the death, knife in the side of the throat. Quite simple, very quiet too. Not a lot of blood, but a lot of air that didn't get into the lungs. She'd have died slowly from suffocation. Not pretty. Quite effective.'

'Professional?' queried Hope.

'I wouldn't go that far,' said Jona. 'Professional may be a bit strong. Keen amateur could do it. You'd have to be fairly strong to hold her though. Certainly, someone who knew what they were doing. I can't find any traces of a person here. I'm searching as much as I can but the grass doesn't help. There's not a lot of indentation. It's quite firm at the moment, fairly dry. If you come over here,' Jona pointed to where one of her assistants was looking at the ground, 'there's definitely a form of indentation. Look at that,' Jona bent down, pointed to a specific hole, a tiny indentation that had made a hole you could pour a very small amount of liquid into. 'What does that look like to you?'

'Looks like somebody put a broom handle, no, the end of a broom handle down on it or some sort of crutch. The round end of a crutch into the ground.'

Jona stood up like she was holding a staff. 'The indentation is not that deep. It's not being lent on. It's more like it's come from the item itself. I'm not sure we got an actual weight for the rod we're looking for.'

'Should be fairly substantial, isn't it? I mean, it was coming from back in the day. Biblical times, the wounds would be quite dense. I guess.'

'Who said it came from back then?' said Jona. 'There's a high likelihood that this item is fairly recent or at best coming from the Middle Ages. It's certainly won't have come from Biblical times.'

'I was trying to keep out of all that. I heard the boss having a go with Clarissa about it. Whatever it is, somebody wants it. I think I'll start to look at it more like a treasure.'

'There's many different sides to it,' said Jona. 'The thing is an artifact, it's not just a piece of art. It's an artifact and people think it's imbued with power. That's a dangerous mix.'

'Is there any indication of a third person being here?' asked Hope.

'I can't tell,' said Jona, 'I really can't. We found this indentation of the staff, it looks like there's a possible foot near it, but it's not deep enough to get anything reasonable from. I've scanned over and around the body, but I can't at the moment get a trace of anything, threads, clothing cotton, anything. I'm really getting nothing here. We'll have to take the body back and see if there's anything in terms of hair or skin, but I'm not holding out much hope.'

Hope stood up and looked around her. 'Why would you come here, Inchnadamph, it's miles from anywhere? We are on the west coast; it'd be much easier to meet in town. Much, much easier.'

'Maybe that was the problem. You could probably see someone coming from miles around here and you weren't going to worry they were a local or just somebody walking past if you were coming here you were coming for a reason. But that is also the problem. If someone was coming and you didn't like it, you wanted out of the situation. Where would you go?

'Everything seems to speak of amateur again, somebody playing without knowing what they were about. If the stuff was here, did that mean they bought it or had they stolen it? But there'd be another body around the corner to find. A body of the person who had actually brought the staff.'

There were too many variables at the moment. In fact, all they had was that people would be looking for the staff. People would want it for power. Some would want it for money. Who it was, Hope had no idea. She thanked Jona and made her way across the small churchyard and into the tiny kirk. Sitting down on one of the wooden benches, she looked up at the front where she saw the small cross on a table.

Hope sat looking around as if an inspiration would suddenly arrive with her. She was going to have to wait until Jona got a bit further on and then she would ring the boss, explain what was happening. Before her on the pew was a Bible, and Hope took it, wondering where the story of Aaron's Rod would be. *It was Moses, wasn't it?*

Quickly she opened up the book, looking for the book of Moses. When she didn't have any luck, she started looking down through the passages. *Old Testament*, she thought. *That was right, wasn't it? Jesus, New Testament, other people Old Testament and it was long ago so we need to start at the beginning.* Except not too far at the beginning because that's when everything was being made. At least that's how she remembered it. Sitting there, she thought again for a moment, and started flicking through the Bible, scanning through the many books inside it, trying to find Moses. The text was small and she could easily miss the word. Putting the Bible down, Hope walked back outside the Church and showed it to Jona.

'Aaron's Rod, what book is it in?'

'The Bible,' shouted Jona, with almost a hint of disgust in her voice.

'I know it's the Bible. What book of the Bible?'

'Exodus,' said an exasperated Jona. 'It's when they're leaving, they go and see Pharaoh. I thought you got taught that in school or RE, or whatever it was.'

'I didn't really pay much attention in RE; I wasn't that sort of kid. I just drew the pictures whenever they told you.' Hope saw Jona smile and made her way back inside. Exodus was the second book in the Bible. She quickly flicked through before lighting on the word Moses and she scanned forward until she saw the name Aaron. Took Hope about half an hour to read and digest the story fully. He was a bit of a cheat really; Moses had asked his brother to turn up and speak for him. A man who wanted to come in and lead everyone needing his brother to do the speaking. Then it was bit far-fetched surely, throwing a rod on the ground, turning into a snake eating other snakes, and then all those plagues as well.

But in her mind, Hope thought that she really needed to see this through the eyes of a zealot, someone who believed this stuff. What could this Rod do at the end of the day? Maybe it wasn't that, maybe it was the power of belief. The power of this force and people who trusted, that was a dangerous mix. One thing Hope couldn't figure out was if this were a staff of God and something that God was in, why would he let it go to somebody who would use it to take over the world? That surely wasn't his idea, was it? His idea was more live and let live. That's what the Jesus guy was about, wasn't it?

In some ways, Hope wished Macleod was there. He could run through and explain what it was to have this faith, what it was to trust. She knew he'd had his problems with it, but at least she might get a better handle on the zealots and why they were thinking what they were thinking. But then again, it could have just been somebody looking for the money. If you've got something everybody wants, you can sell it to the highest bidder. The other question remained, if this were such an artifact, such a relic and built with such power and something that was not unheard of—after all, Clarissa spotted it almost immediately—why would you dress it up and hide it? Why not just sell it at Sotheby's or whatever other auctioneers, the big ones down in London? Why sell it at a little start-up and in Invershin? It seemed that who then bought it was killed for it. This didn't make sense, why would you buy it to then turn up to meet someone else. You don't randomly get killed out here; you don't randomly find Inchnadamph.

We need to go back to the auction, thought Hope. *We need to get behind that. Ross needs to get back and get those statements sorted.*

88

Chapter 11

'So, where are we exactly?' asked Macleod. He was standing up, looking out of the window of his office and behind him, his small team were sitting around the conference desk in his office. The finding of the second body had somewhat intensified the hunt through the records from the auction house, and Ross, on his return from Inchnadamph, had been pouring through transcriptions of interviews uniform had conducted with people who had been at the auction. Clarissa joined him to give some know-how on how an auction worked.

'From what we can tell,' said Ross, 'there was a couple who bought the Rod in the auction. It seemed to go for quite a low price—had extraordinarily little interest in it, at least on the day. It had gone up briefly online only to be taken down, and then reappear the day before the auction. From the descriptions given by the public at the auction, it seems that the couple from the hotel are likely candidates to have bought the Rod. With what we found in Inchnadamph, it would seem that it's more than likely.'

'I think we can read a lot more into it than that,' said Clarissa.

'In what way?' asked Macleod.

'Well,' said Clarissa, 'the item goes up into the auction catalogue only to be taken down. It then sits there until the day before when it's suddenly back on the table. That sounds like someone trying to put it out there to be bought on the quiet. The thing is, Inspector, if this item was seen, there would be a lot of interest, both normal interest and untoward interest who would pay a large price tag for it.'

'Why wouldn't you just put it up in an auction?' asked Macleod. 'Why not just put it there?'

'Exactly,' said Clarissa. 'That's what's strange about this. If I were the auctioneer, at least any normal auctioneer, I'd be wanting to advertise this everywhere. Take what? A 10% cut? I wouldn't be surprised if you couldn't sell that item for at least a million, if not more. In fact, it could go for a lot more. It's difficult to even put a value on it. You'd have museums looking for it, as well as private collectors. Yet, it's in the catalogue as a rather drab walking stick.'

'Could it be that the auctioneer was incompetent?' asked Hope.

Clarissa stood up, much to Macleod's annoyance, and he watched her pace back and forward across the room deep in thought.

'Look, I know you people don't understand auction houses and that, but this is not normal. I'm trying to get my head around this. I've done a little bit of background research into Forrest Mackenzie. As far as auction houses go and as an auctioneer, he's not got a long history. He's more a buyer and seller. In fact, I'm trying to work out why on earth he's opened up an auction house. He seems to have the nuance to find expensive items and sell them on.'

'Are you saying that somebody might not have brought the

item to him, he might have found it and then put it in an auction?' asked Hope. 'That seems a rather backward way of doing it. If somebody had an item and they didn't know what it was, surely, he would just turn around and say, "I'll give you fifty quid for that. Take it, go and flog it somewhere else", and that'll be legit and above board, wouldn't it?' asked Hope.

'It would, completely, and that's what's bothering me.'

'There is something else you need to know,' said Ross. 'At the auction house, there was an online side, so you wouldn't just be selling to the room, you could be selling to the world. Now, according to what records we can take out from the computer systems, there were bids being made initially for this item, and they were online. According to the public in the room, there was only one couple bidding for it in the room, certainly once it got past £100. There was someone before that, an elderly gentleman, but he dropped out pretty quick. By the sounds of it, he was a genuine buyer who had no idea that this was more than a walking stick. However, online, the bids came in extremely large.'

'How large?' asked Macleod.

'Half a million,' said Ross. 'That was for starters. The strange thing is then, that the internet link dropped off. Basically, anyone bidding online had been voided because they couldn't get the system back up.'

'Wouldn't you just wait?' asked Macleod, looking at Clarissa. The woman was still marching back and forward, her hand running through her purple hair.

'You would, Inspector. You could pause it for certainly five or ten minutes and ask the question, see if you could get the link back. If it were an extremely important item that you were selling for a lot of money, yes, you would, but if you didn't want

91

to sell it for a lot of money, then maybe, just maybe, you would cut that link.'

'It seems to me,' said Macleod, 'that Forrest Mackenzie is trying to sell the item for as little as possible to certain people, but why?'

Clarissa suddenly looked like she had a moment of inspiration. 'Als, give me that transcript.'

'Which one?' asked Ross.

'The younger woman. What was she called? Frances something—she describes the bidding. Give me it now.'

Ross handed it over, and Macleod made his way behind Clarissa, staring over her shoulder as she scanned the document.

'Find anything?' asked Macleod.

'This woman describes the two making the bids, the man and the woman in the room. The woman is probably now dead. She says that they're not making it from excitement, said it was very mundane, almost matter of fact. There was no excitement from them when they won, which would lead you to think they didn't know what the item was, or they knew they were going to win. She also describes that the auctioneer had a look of fright on his face. I think that's around about the time that the internet bids came in. She says it wasn't long after that that he actually made an apology that the internet was down, and therefore, bidding was all in the room.

'What are we saying?' asked Macleod.

'That's obvious, isn't it?' said Clarissa. 'For some reason, this Rod had to go into an auction house. Why, we don't know, but what we do know is that once it's gone in, our auctioneer has made sure that certain people bought it and bought it for next to nothing.'

'Where is his cut then?' asked Hope.

'His cut will be when they sell it. They'll sell it on and he will then pick up a large chunk of that. They've hid it. They've tried to do it on the quiet, possibly because they knew the attention it would bring.'

'How hard would it be to know,' asked Macleod, 'that this was Aaron's Rod and not just a staff?'

Clarissa looked up at her new boss and smiled. 'Well, think about it. I'm not a complete expert in this field. Yes, I've got a passing knowledge and a good understanding, but I spotted it. Anybody that's actively looking for it, searching the internet, trying to find things, and they do, trust me, they do, they have been onto it straightaway. Even the short time span of just a day, they've obviously found it and the bids have come in. Maybe they couldn't get there in time.'

'Then when they couldn't, somebody's come and had a talk with the auctioneer,' said Hope, 'but that means—'

'Somebody's hunting them down,' said Macleod. 'We've got people on the trail here. Ross, those internet connections, were you able to find out where they came from, the bids?'

'We tried following the line back, sir,' said Ross, 'but it's not happening. They're bouncing about from servers from here to there, according to the tech department. They're still working on it, but I doubt they're going to get anywhere.'

'Well, that's a problem then,' said Macleod. 'What do we do then? How do we follow this?'

'Well, it's quite obvious that we've got to find the other man from the couple,' said Hope. 'I know Jona's going to come up with something.'

'If we can trace the last movements of our auctioneer,' said Macleod, 'we might have a hope, get into the past, see who he talked to. You said that this Rod had to go to auction house for some reason. We need that reason, Clarissa. You need to get back into your contacts. Find out what was going on. I assume also that if this item had come up, there'd be noise, a lot of noise about it. It's something that's so precious, according to yourself, something that people want bad enough to kill for.'

'Very much so,' said Clarissa, 'very much.' The woman looked quite shaken. Almost as if something had dawned on her. Seeing the look on her face, Macleod turned to his other two colleagues.

'I think that's it,' he said. 'Ross, get back onto the tech department; see if they can get through on those internet lines. Hope, you get back onto the couple; see if you can get any further on that. Also, check in on Jona. I want to know if any evidence has been found up at Inchnadamph, anything we can use, and confirm the ID on that girl, the dead one.' Hope nodded and stood up from the desk, followed by Ross. The silent dismissal had been given, and they made their way out the door. Clarissa went to follow them.

'Just a moment,' said Macleod. 'Shut the door behind them, would you?'

The woman did as asked and then turned with quite a solemn face.

'Something wrong, Inspector?'

'You tell me,' said Macleod. 'I'd have thought at the moment, you'd have been jumping all over this. It's right in your field. It's what we asked you here for, and you've nailed it. You've sorted the problem. You've told us where we need to go to find out where this Rod comes from. You told us about other interested parties. We have the Lord Argyles and others of this world chasing it down too, but something about you tells me you're bothered. Something isn't right.'

'Tell me, Inspector,' said Clarissa, 'when you see these bodies, when people die, how do you feel?'

'That's a rather serious question.'

'It is, and it's one that keeps coming to mind. You must have seen plenty of dead bodies in your time as a police officer.'

'Well, yes. I've worked at the murder department for most of my career. It kind of comes with the territory.'

'What does it do to you?'

Macleod took a seat behind his desk and pointed Clarissa to the chair in front of it, offering her a seat.

'Sit down. You have to get used to it. Although, you never really do get used to it. You have to be able to move it to one side. Deal with the fascination of the little intricacies. Try to see the people behind, not the horror of the killing. Try to think about what's going on, not just dwell on the dark side of it.'

'And what? It doesn't bother you?' said Clarissa. 'You can just go on?'

'Never,' said Macleod. 'If anybody comes through this side of our work and isn't affected by it, there's something wrong. Why are you asking? You weren't at Inchnadamph. Granted, you saw Mackenzie and his body in the auction house.'

'It's not that. I have seen a body before, but with the cases I worked, we didn't tend to get that many. Sometimes people kill for artwork, but generally not. Some people might get threatened, beaten up, but it's not what's bothering me.'

'What's bothering you,' said Macleod, 'is the fact that whether or not somebody else tonight gets murdered, somebody else gets found and killed partly rests on your shoulders. You need to come up with the goods or somebody dies. I guess that's rather different to simply losing a piece of artwork.'

Clarissa looked at Macleod, staring, her chin almost wobbling as she went to speak. 'It scares the living daylights out of me, Seoras; if I don't get this right, if I don't get on top of this, because let's be honest, that's why I'm here, to get on top of this. You need my expertise, but if I don't come through with the goods, somebody else dies.' Macleod stepped up, walked round his desk, and put his hands Clarissa's shoulders, and felt her begin to shake.

'I can't take that away. It's what we do. It's how we work. It's what we have to go with. I'd say, if it was too much for you, just to go, but I need you. I need your knowledge in this case. I'm in a world I neither understand nor have any experience of. I'm also an officer down, the one who could ferret, get underneath the skin of things to see what was really going on. I think you can do that, but if you need me, I'm here,' said Macleod. 'We don't do this alone. We do this together. All four of us. So, any issues, any difficulties, you come to us. We'll get you through it. Then afterwards, we'll get you through that as well. Now, go find me something. I want to know who those interested parties were, and I want to know how he got that Rod.'

'Yes, Inspector, of course. I'm sorry. It's just—'

'There's no need to apologize. It doesn't get any easier with time. You just learn to have more of a poker face.'

Clarissa stood up, gave a sniff, and walked over to the door. As she placed her hand on it, she turned back to Macleod. 'Do you drink?' she said.

'No. Never,' said Macleod.

'What gets you through? How do you cope with this?'

'The rest of the team will tell you it's my fun and cheery disposition and the ability to laugh at things at all times that does it.'

Clarissa smiled and turned away, and then stopped and looked back.

'That was a joke, wasn't it?' she said.

'Yes, it was. I get through by getting through, and sometimes, I don't get through very well. Now, go get me what I need.'

Chapter 12

C larissa stood in the darkness, a shawl wrapped up around her. The time was midnight, and she was waiting for a contact who she had last spoken to some ten years ago. Her evening had been spent ringing around numerous people, seeing if anyone had heard of any news about Aaron's Rod. Most people had been quiet, many difficult to gauge. Did they know something, or were they just keeping out of it?

It seemed that the item was hot in demand, and this contact she was to meet had spoken of it in a very negative way, but Clarissa had insisted he gave her every detail because of what she knew about him. The man had committed a criminal misdemeanour that had been let go because of information that he had passed to Clarissa. Of course, she'd never let that hold disappear, and as soon as he tried to clam up and say nothing about the item, Clarissa had demanded an audience with him. The fact he was looking to meet at a bus shelter on a road out of Dingwall at midnight said something about the fear the item was causing to the man.

The particular bit of road he'd suggested was unlit, and Clarissa had wondered if she should bring somebody to accompany her, but if the man had seen them, he would have run off. There was a light breeze blowing, and despite being closer to summer than winter, Clarissa was feeling the cold at this late hour. Maybe that was due to her age. She certainly found the older she got, the colder she began to feel. Back in her younger days, she had thought nothing of drifting along on a night like this, no jacket, possibly even a short skirt, but these days she was wrapped up in a tight shawl.

'You really don't want in on this one,' said a voice behind her. Clarissa didn't flinch, but instead just stared ahead. The particular bus shelter she was in was of modern type with a narrow plastic-covered seat running from one side to the other with clear plastic all the way around it. However, the sheet behind her had been smashed with part of it being removed. It was through this gap that the voice was coming, her contact deciding not to be visible from the road.

'Is this essential? It is rather cold out here today, darling.' Clarissa was aware she was going to have to put on an antique character, one she had used for many years. The man was unaware that she was actually a detective, thinking instead that she had links to the force without being a policewoman herself. That was why the threat of revealing his misdemeanour to them held such weight. 'It's an item I'm after,' said Clarissa. 'I think the price is worth the risk.'

'If you think your life is worth it, you're more of a fool than I ever thought you for.' The man's voice was harsh, but Clarissa could hear the tremble in it.

'Why do you know of it? Where's this information coming from?' asked Clarissa. 'I need to know it's good. I don't want to walk into a shambles. That time in Perth, that was shoddy, that was.' Clarissa was referring to a previous time when information gathered had led to a rather embarrassing lift of the wrong individuals. 'I nearly lost my good credentials over that.'

'Don't worry, this is good.'

The contact behind Clarissa was only known to her as Angus. His surname had never been revealed to her, although she believed it was Morrison. In truth, she wasn't that bothered. The man was a fixer, a mover of things. That was why she reckoned he would be contacted if the plans to sell the Rod had gone south. After all, the auctioneer who had obviously set up some sort of scam was dead. The woman involved in the scheme was now dead as well, so the man looking to run with the item may also be looking to get rid of it quickly.

'What happened? Where is this Rod?'

'I got contacted.'

'Who by?'

'Third Party of a third party, and that's all you're getting.' The man coughed. Clarissa thought it was because his voice was becoming a little choked up. 'I also had a visit from certain people in higher places. Made sure that it wasn't something I wanted to take on.'

Higher places was code. In the past, Clarissa had dealings with Lord Argyle and most of his network. Angus Morrison, her contact, had often run items for him. They had a good working relationship, but one that was also top-heavy, in that when Argyle said something or told Angus not to take on something, he didn't.

'Is Argyle after the rod? That's going to complicate things,' said Clarissa. 'I'll have to go out on the quiet.'

'Well, he won't get it out through me. I am hands-off. If he finds out I've even been talking to you, well, let's say I probably won't walk right for a few weeks.' Clarissa knew that the threat was real and that her contact was not simply being dramatic.

'What can you tell me?'

'I know they were worried,' said the man. 'Somebody else was after it, too. I think there's a trade being made. All I'm saying is our guy wasn't happy. Looks like he's behind the curve on this.'

'That's it? You just stepped out? That's not like you. You'd want to know what was going on. Did you ask around?'

'You're not getting anything else,' said the man.

'You're out here because you know what I know about you. You know where I can take that. This isn't some minor thing. This isn't some little antic. This could set me up for life,' said Clarissa. 'I want to know where it is.'

'I did speak to some others. I did hear something, but it's just a rumour that's not a widely known rumour.'

'Do the higher-up people know this rumour?'

'No. No, they don't. They say there's a bigger player involved. They said there's going to be a handover. Somebody's going to be taking it to run with it.'

'When? Where?'

'I didn't hear.'

'Of course, you heard. You don't get that unfinished information without knowing about it. In fact, you set it up, didn't you? It's no wonder you're scared. Argyle will kill you if he knows that.'

'Yes, well—'

'Yes, well, nothing. You need to tell me where it is so I can go and make my bet on it.'

'It hardly matters,' said the man. 'You're not getting there in time anyway.'

'How do you mean?' asked Clarissa.

'They're meeting up at Ardvreck Castle anytime now, maybe an hour's time. That's where the handover is happening. You're not getting there. It's too far out of the way.'

'That's why you're here. That's why you made me wait this late,' said Clarissa. 'I might just dump you in it anyway.'

'Dump me in if you like, but I'm still alive and out of this. Don't dare breathe a word about it. This is big—you know it is. Maybe you can go and see them when they make the trade up there. Get involved. Personally, I'm keeping out of it. They say there's two dead already.'

'Who does?'

'Those higher up.'

'Did they kill them? Did he kill them?'

'He doesn't tell me that sort of thing. He always implies it was him, but you can't be sure, can you? That's the way it works, isn't it? Intimidation, being on top. I wouldn't put it past him though.'

Clarissa breathed deeply. Lord Argyle was heavily involved. The case was taking on another element. There were two interested parties online. Had the original man and woman and Forrest Mackenzie had somewhere to go to, somewhere to sell, or were they going to put it up as a secret bid? Maybe they'd been right amateur about it, made a mess of it, and now everyone was after them. She wouldn't know, not unless she found the man to talk to, got in on this. Clarissa turned back over her shoulder.

'Ardvreck Castle, is that correct?' There was silence behind her. Getting up, she walked around the back of the bus shelter and found no one there. *The wee sod*, thought Clarissa. *Dammit. I'm going to need to call this in*, she thought. *What's the time?*

He's got it right; we're going to miss it. Dammit. Clarissa picked up her mobile phone and called Macleod's number.

* * *

Hope had been up in Inchnadamph with Ross, talking to some of the local policemen and seeing if they could find any other route to check in to see if Forrest Mackenzie had been up and around the area. It was a somewhat strange out-of-the-way place on the road to Lochinver, and Hope had wondered if that's the area the staff had originally come from. She was heading back down to the station, wondering if they'd get there before one in the morning, when she got the call from Macleod. Instantly, she'd spun the car around.

'Where are we going?' asked Ross.

'Ardvreck Castle,' said Hope. 'Clarissa's had a tip. There's a meeting there. Possibly the Rod being handed over. Who knows? But she said it's going to be tight. We may not get there in time, so buckle up.'

Ross put his left hand up, grabbing the handle above the door, as Hope raced along the small country roads. Ardvreck Castle was a ruined fifteenth-century fortification just north of Inchnadamph and sat on the side of Loch Assynt. At this time of night, there was little light around it. Hope made her way to the car park and found no cars there making her wonder if this might be a damp squib, a ruse made to send them off track. She parked up and, together with Ross, made their way along the small path towards Ardvreck Castle.

As they approached in the darkness, the cloud cover meant that it was difficult to see anything and keeping their foot on the path was difficult enough. Hope found herself having to use her pen torch, pointing it down towards her feet to make sure they got their footing. The path made its way towards the beach that sat beside the castle, and from there, the pair were able to walk up towards the stone structure. There was a stiff breeze blowing, making it hard to hear anything around them. Together, they slowly edged up towards the castle. As they made their way up the small hill, Hope thought she could hear voices and indicated to Ross that he should quieten down. Slowly, they went around the perimeter of the castle, watching their footing on the unsteady terrain. As they came to the far side, the voices became more distinct.

'Where is it then?' said a woman's voice. Hope thought the voice sounded cold, sharp, and nasally. She wondered what sort of woman it would be. The voice was older and confident.

'It's in a safe place,' said a man, but there was a wavering in the voice.

'It should be out here. Why would I want it to be anywhere else? It should be out here. You make a deal, you bring it with you.'

'I was warned about you. Have you got the money with you?'

'The money's in a safe place, son,' said the woman. 'I guess you've left the item with your associate.' Hope heard a gasp. 'Yes, I know you had more than one. She told me that before I killed her.'

'You won't get it from her. I want the money. I want the money first.'

'I don't need the money anymore. I know he has it, so that's where I'll go. Thank you for your assistance. It's been good to know you. You've been very inventive, but you should learn to cover your back better than that.'

Hope could hear the threat in the voice and could hear the

situation going south. The man, for whatever reason, clearly was not used to playing this sort of game. In such a place, there was no backup for him, no one to hear anything untoward happening to him. He was fortunate that this night, Hope was just around the corner.

'Police. Stand down. Everyone, face down on the ground,' shouted Hope. She'd done this on the premise that most people would think they were surrounded by a large number of people. When you can't see the police that are coming to arrest you, you assume the worst. At least most people do. Instead, a shot rang out in the night. Hope threw herself to the floor, looking around in the dark, trying to see the two figures.

'Alan, are you okay?'

'Fine.'

Hope heard feet disappearing away from the castle, somebody running hard. She decided not to turn on her pen torch, instead making her way around the edge of the castle wall where she tumbled over something, falling to the ground. Heading away from her beyond the castle, she could see a figure running. It was indistinct, but she saw the shadow moving.

'What's your foot on? There's something here.' With that, Hope put on her torch and swept it back. Her eyes first saw the blood, and then it swept quickly past part of a head. She quickly looked to see a face, one she had seen on a screen from a hotel CCTV, but which was now severely disfigured.

'God, she's killed him. She's killed him. Quick. We need to get after her.'

'She's got a gun, Hope. Careful.'

Hope wasn't listening, and instead took off in the dark to follow the woman. Watching the woman, or rather, her shadows, she disappeared back along the beach before cutting off and across the road that ran up the side of the castle. Hope was in good shape and continued to run hard and was beginning to find herself gaining ground.

Maybe the woman was older. She certainly didn't look as agile as Hope. On the far side of the road was a small river running down the side of a hill. Hope watched the woman making her way up through it. There were no large drops, and Hope ran through the riverbed, her Doc Martens splashing through the cold water.

Ahead, everything was dark, and she had to concentrate on her feet below her, looking out for any undue rocks. Several times, she stumbled but all the while, she found herself gaining ground on the woman. She was maybe one hundred metres behind now, and then she looked up. She thought the shadow of the woman had stopped. Hope continued getting closer, but then something in her made her pause for a moment. Why was the woman not moving? Why was she not trying to get away? Hope threw herself to the ground. A shot rang out through the night. Hope lay down in the stream but could not stop herself rising up to see her target. Behind the woman was a crashing waterfall, and she disappeared into the darkness of the foliage around it. Hope went to follow but a second shot drove her back.

The woman's shadow had gone. With no way of knowing where the woman was, Hope would be a prime target for the gun. Slowly, eyes peeled on where the woman had vanished to, Hope made her way back down the riverbed.

Chapter 13

H ope looked shaken as she sat drinking coffee at the conference table the next morning. Macleod was watching her from behind his desk, while Clarissa and Ross were conversing loudly, clearly with thoughts on what to do about the investigation. The Inspector was feeling worried for his team, three people were now dead, all in pursuit of Aaron's Rod, but at the moment, the only thing Macleod had was a basic idea about who was after it. Clarissa's contact had indicated there were two parties, not just one, and that bothered Macleod more than anything. There could be some sort of war over this. At least if it was one party and they got the Rod that would be that, the killings would stop, but with a war on or at least some type of deadly tussle, Macleod was worried that the number of bodies was going to go up. Clearly, a number of people in the art world were not happy and staying out of harm's way, but money always attracted people. Money always brought those into the line of fire, who normally would stay clear.

Macleod stood up and asked his team if anyone needed a coffee before making his way outside to the main office where the filter machine sat on the far side. He returned with two cups putting one in front of Hope and took his place at the head of the table.

'Last night's shooter, what do we know about her, Hope?' asked Macleod.

'I didn't get a good look at her, Ross didn't either. It was too dark sir, too dark; we didn't find her car either. Pretty hard to find someone like that, despite the fact that uniform got out and started stopping cars on the road.'

'She definitely doesn't have the Rod, does she?'

'No,' said Hope. 'I believe there was meant to be an exchange there, of money for the Rod, but clearly that wasn't going to happen. Someone of importance was after this. People just don't turn around and start gunning people down. That's quite high power.'

Macleod saw her shake when she said it. 'How close did you get?' asked Macleod.

'It was close,' said Ross. 'Too close, several shots, one at a time. We were operating in the dark.'

'We need to take a look at ourselves,' said Macleod. 'We need to make sure we're not running an undue risk here. This is a stick; it's not a person we're trying to save—just a stick.'

'With all due respect, Inspector,' said Clarissa, 'people are going to get injured if we don't find this object and quick, I think we're all aware of that.'

'Those people getting injured will have chosen to be part of this, Detective. As far as this team goes, don't put yourself in unnecessary risk. That was foolish, Hope. Last night was foolish. You saw her, she had a gun, she used it to deadly effect; to chase off into the dark after her, you're lucky to be here.'

Hope nodded and Ross put a hand on her shoulder. 'I think she's very aware of that, Inspector.'

'But where does it leave us?' asked Macleod. 'Clarissa, what about your contact? Any more on that side?'

'He's not going to come forward with anything about that side of the operation. He's under threat from them anyway. He doesn't want them to know that I knew about him. In fact, he's probably gone to ground at this point in time because they'll want to know how we got there.'

'But you do suspect Lord Argyle? Is that still the case?'

'Definitely,' said Clarissa. 'My contact was pretty adamant about it coming up from on high and that's who he's referring to. I would suggest that we start putting a little bit more heat on him.'

'But we haven't got anything on him,' said Macleod. 'That's going to be hard to wear. Someone like that will have a good lawyer.'

'Not on him specifically, on the organization, on the people around him. A man like him doesn't come out of the dark unless there's something worth getting. Therefore, he'll have his people running around looking for this initially. I would suspect he'd only come to it if he has to. Although, given what it is, he might want to be the first one to have hold of it.'

'Well, in that case, you and I will do it,' said Macleod. 'I think you could do with a day here at the station, Hope. Take Ross and get back into looking through the records. Get into that sale and find out who was the initial person to own the Rod. Who brought the Rod to Forrest Mackenzie? I think there's part of this we're not getting. Clarissa and I will try and get some heat on Lord Argyle. Unless Jona comes up with something else, I'm not sure it's going to be a phenomenally successful day.'

'Forensic reported on the weapon from last night, sir,' said

Ross. 'Indicated that it was a common bullet. Doubt we're going to trace it to the gun, if indeed the gun is still about.'

'She's probably disposed of the weapon,' said Hope.

'Would you say she was professional?' asked Macleod.

'She didn't hesitate,' said Hope. 'Once she knew something was up, she just killed him. There's definitely a professional edge there.'

'Okay, both of you get onto it. See if you can find me who that vendor is. Also, coordinate some stop and search out in that part of the country. Given the time of day it happened, I doubt anybody's going to know anything, but anything suspicious, anything untoward that's been seen by the public comes back here, comes through me. Is that understood?'

'Perfectly,' said Ross.

Ross and Hope made their way out of Macleod's office into the main area while Clarissa remained at the table.

'You okay?' asked Macleod.

'No,' said Clarissa. 'But we need to move on this. It won't be easy, especially finding a trace through to Argyle. The number of times I've tried in our other dealings, and I've never been able to do it.'

'Maybe not,' said Macleod. 'But at the end of the day, you said this is more than just a piece of art. For some people this is, well, God's Rod, God's staff. They're looking for mystical powers in it. I mean, would he kill for a piece of art?'

'Not so openly in my experience. The man has certainly been behind some things, some very distasteful, but I've never known it to be this extreme. Of course, if it is to do with the mythological side of the item, he won't be alone.'

'It seems rather fancy if you will. I mean, you're seriously telling me these people meet and try and bring these things together? That they actually have some society to try and find these items?'

'Trust me, Inspector.'

'Where do we start then?' asked Macleod.

'Argyle uses certain private investigators,' said Clarissa. 'I happen to know who most of them are. It's a way of keeping your head in the game. Most of them talk to you if they don't think you're Police. He'll use several different ones. That's what he does so none of them have the big picture, but they'll have something. I think with a bit of pressure from us, we can get plenty out of them.'

Macleod stood up. 'They're bound to be scared when they hear what's going down. Let's hope they talk.'

'Depends what you have got on people if they'll talk or not. I'm sure we can find plenty.'

'Okay,' said Macleod. 'Grab your coat and let's get moving. We need to start making headway quickly. Otherwise, the DCI is going to be on top of me.'

* * *

Ross tried to focus on his work but sitting behind his desk, he kept looking across at his boss, Sergeant McGrath, who seemed to be struggling.

'He was right, wasn't he?' asked Hope.

'Who?' asked Ross.

'The boss. I shouldn't have run after her. I shouldn't have chased her down like that; it was a bit reckless.'

'It was downright reckless,' said Ross. 'Especially with what she was carrying. We don't normally chase after people who are carrying, probably lucky to be here this morning. She didn't hesitate in killing that guy.'

'No, she didn't, did she? Jona got any way of identifying that couple from their bodies?'

'Not so far; they're not on fingerprint record. We were checking through missing persons, but nothing's coming back. I reckon these people keep themselves on a low profile. They'll be there to pass it on to someone there to make the deal. People like that live in the background,' said Ross.

'We may never find out who they are. Unless we can find someone we know who's been dealing with them, but that's awkward. Forrest Mackenzie's dead, we can't find the vendor so far, and, well, whoever they were talking to you doesn't want to talk to them now. They killed them. That's if they would have even known their names.' Hope nodded, but was shifting uneasily on her seat.

'Are you all right?' asked Ross.

'No, I'm not. Damn it, I could have been killed last night. I can't relax, I can't sit still thinking about it.'

'Go for a run or something, or go punch something down the gym. Go on, take half an hour, I've got this covered here. I can't work with you jumping about in front of me.'

Hope laughed at him, 'Okay,' she said, 'half an hour only. I'll be back and you better have made some progress by then; otherwise, Macleod is going to ring our necks.'

Ross grinned and watched his boss stand up and leave the room. As she went, he bent back down to his computer gazing at the screen. For the last hour and a half, he'd been searching through the records from the sale at the auction house. Tracing back here and there for anything, but nothing was coming up. The vendor was never mentioned, no one else appeared to have anything to do with the item, except for the couple who bought it and Forrest Mackenzie.

Ross decided a new tactic needed to be employed. Forensics had produced photographs of the item, provided by Jona, and Ross tried to get a match through the various social media channels. It was a long painstaking process, and in fact, for a large part of the time, he had to sit there and let the computer work away. Granted, it came up with matches and he looked at a number of posts on social media. All were walking sticks or some sort of staff. One was an ornate staff from a drama production about the Egyptians, another was taken at a sheepdog trial. Ross started scanning, stick after stick, crook after crook, staff after staff until eventually, he felt that his eyes had become crossed. As he took his cup of coffee and drunk it, he wondered if he was doing a futile search.

He didn't catch the item at first as it sailed past down the screen and off the bottom, but something in him made him roll the screen back up. He recognized the colours, the jewels on the staff, even if it looked slightly dishevelled, and a lot muckier than it should. Ross stared at it for several minutes and picked up an image of what Aaron's Rod should look like. Bit by bit he matched each jewel from his reference picture to that on the screen. He took a look across at where the post had come from and found out it was a Facebook one. He clicked on the account and looked over to see the name Howie Lemon and a number of pictures about metal detecting. Ross could feel his heart skip a beat.

This was it. This must have been the guy that found it. Slowly, he scrolled through the daily messages from the man. He didn't seem to have a lot of interaction on his page—the occasional like, the odd daft comment, but every three or four pictures, he had a metal detector in hand. Then Ross hit upon one where there was a hole in the ground and beside it lay the staff, Aaron's Rod covered in muck. It didn't say where the find had happened, or maybe that was something to protect Howie from any repeat visitors. People who would get in there and detect ahead of him in case there were any more relics in the ground.

Ross knew he had a lead now, and he quickly picked up the phone to try and get details of the man on the screen. Howie had crazy, curly hair but there was a grin in the man's eye at every object he seemed to have picked up. Yet, the post was so dull as if written by somebody incredibly simple. It would be difficult for Ross to get a search of the man's house. He'd probably need to go to a sheriff, Scotland's judges, in order for that to happen. He kept scrolling through and realized that the man lived in the local area. The only indication on the screen was the stated location; it said Scotland. But Ross began to coordinate whereabouts Howie was from by seeing the locations of where things had been found from the pictures given.

Occasional photographs of trips out, where they'd started from, made Ross realize that most were villages in the local area. He then looked at the picture on either side of the find and saw a common point. Checking the phonebook for the area, Ross looked up Lemon and found a number. The address came up on the computer beside the phone number. It tallied with the pictures either side of the find.

Ross leaped up from his desk, ran down to the small gym in the basement of the station. As he opened the door, he saw a treadmill spinning fast. Hope dressed in her Lycra, not simply running, but almost sprinting on the device. She didn't even ask what, instead simply hitting the automatic stop button before jumping off the treadmill.

'Two minutes, Ross, I'll be with you in two minutes.' After

working with him for so long, Hope clearly knew this was something big.

Chapter 14

'I don't take kindly to sitting in a hedge,' said Macleod.

'Well, if you want, I can do this on my own. I guess it's been a while since you didn't have somebody else to do the legwork.'

'I'll have you know I can do the legwork as well as anyone.'

'I know,' said Clarissa, 'I heard. Fort Augustus. Left your partner in a hospital to come and sort it out. That kind of thing gets around.'

'Well,' said Macleod, 'needs must, but I still don't see why I'm sitting in a hedge at the moment.'

'You will. Lord Argyle uses a number of people, various investigators, but like most people, he has his go-to guys when certain things need done. He would've needed to get someone good who can trace people quickly. Not only that, but he's familiar with the art world. He's used this man many times before. I've even had the odd run-in, but I could never quite nail him on anything. He knows who I am, or rather, he thinks he knows who I am. Cara Lee, collector of antiquities. Quite a shock he's going to get when he finds out I'm a detective.'

'Well, if that's the shock, why am I here?' asked Macleod.

'Because when he realizes there's a DI on the case, and not

only that, it's Macleod, it'll run a cold chill up him. We're going to need to because he won't speak. Well, not much.'

'I could haul him in for you,' said Macleod.

'Then he definitely won't speak. More than that, they'll know something is up. They'll cover their tracks. You'd be putting the man into harm's way. But as much as I don't like him, it's not really our code of conduct, is it?'

'Indeed, it isn't,' said Macleod. 'I'm glad you don't simply fly by night.'

'I didn't get to stay this long in the job without knowing a few tricks or without knowing my limits. Now, quiet, Inspector. It looks like him in the distance.'

Macleod saw a man in a grey pair of flannels with a white shirt and a bizarre baseball jacket over the top. He looked nothing like an antique dealer. In fact, he looked extremely dishevelled. If Macleod hadn't been told by Clarissa that this man was an investigator, Macleod wouldn't have a clue who he was and probably would have suspected him to be some sort of drunk. The man even stumbled a few times, swaying from side to side, and it was only when the man plonked himself on the bench some fifteen feet away from Macleod, that he saw the accuracy with which the man sat. There was no inebriation. The man was perfectly sober and playing a part extremely well. Macleod saw Clarissa's nod and followed her out of the hedge.

'Cara, delightful,' said the man, and then he spotted Macleod behind her, 'but you've brought company. That wasn't on the cards. Don't remember you mentioning that.'

'Just an interested colleague,' said Clarissa. 'Tell me, what have you been up to?'

The man looked at her. 'What sort of a question is that to ask? As if I was going to tell you.'

Clarissa laughed, and turned around, and pushed Macleod's shoulder. 'Lighten up. He's okay, this one,' and then she turned back to the investigator. 'His name is Harry but he calls himself Diggory.' Macleod saw the man's face frown. 'It's always been Diggory to you, Cara. What's with this?'

'A simple question,' said Clarissa, and sat down right beside the man staring up into his face. 'I asked what you've been doing. Working for your lord and master again?'

'If I had been, and I'm not saying I had, you don't think I'd tell you, would you?'

'I think I might be looking for the same man,' said Clarissa. 'Do you think he paid you well?'

'He always pays well,' said Diggory, 'but you still haven't told me how you know my name, my real name.'

'Well, I guess I have one up on you. You see, this time it's serious, isn't it?'

The private investigator nodded. 'It certainly is that. That's why we take things incredibly carefully. He put a tail on me the other day. Imagine that, Cara? A tail. I had to shake him off. Who tails an investigator they've hired? They paid me to find someone.'

'Did you?'

'I always do. That's why you come to me, Cara. You know I'm the best. But he's never done that to Diggory before. Why tail me? Why keep an eye?'

'It's in case you tail off somewhere else,' said Clarissa. 'He's probably scared you might go to the police, might tell them. Who was the man he asked you to trace anyway?'

'I don't know him. I still don't know his name, but he moved along with a woman. They're over on the west side,' said Diggory. 'Found them underneath a little church, or at least her.'

'And then what?' asked Clarissa.

'You're awfully nosy today. Are you looking for them, too?'

'Well, they do have an item, don't they?'

'I don't think they'll have it anymore,' said Diggory. 'I think he's probably taken it off them by now.' The man was staring at Clarissa, trying to eye her up, work out just what she was looking for. Harry leaned forward, looking past Clarissa at Macleod. 'Who is this?'

'The real question, Diggory, is who am I?' said Clarissa. The man frowned, puzzled.

'Why do you say that?' he said. 'I've known you for years. You've always worked your way around the antiques business. You know your stuff. Helped each other occasionally, haven't we? I mean, we're friends.'

'I prefer the term acquaintances,' said Clarissa. 'It's the thing about acquaintances, you're never quite sure who they are. They're always there saying hello, but you're never quite sure.' She saw the panic on the man's face. He turned this way and that looking around him and then went to get up, but Clarissa put a hand on his knee, a firm hand, one that said don't move. 'I thought you'd lost your tail. You worried they're still with you?'

'What's this all about?' asked Diggory.

'It's about dead bodies. It's about the fact that Lord Argyle seems to be operating well above what he's done before. Why is he after it, Diggory?'

'I won't talk about him. As you said, dead bodies.'

'In that case, let me introduce you to some people. The man sitting behind me is Detective Inspector Macleod.'

Clarissa saw the recognition on the man's face. 'Macleod?'

he said, 'You mean the guy I've seen in the papers? There were those killings in Inverness, Christmas time. Then there was that one on the pole by the A9. What's he want with me?' asked Diggory.

'What he wants is for you to tell him who you were looking for, where you found who you were looking for, and what Lord Argyle's up to. And I'd like you to do it too,' Clarissa reached inside her jacket pocket and pulled out a wallet, 'because you see, my name's Detective Sergeant Clarissa Urquhart. I've worked undercover with you for a number of years, feeding off you, learning things, but right now, I'm working with the murder squad and we have bodies falling, bodies all associated with the antiques world, all associated with Aaron's Rod.'

'Shh,' said the man, 'don't. Don't say it. Nobody's meant to know he's looking for it.'

'Well, that genie's out of the box,' said Macleod, 'but what's to stop me lifting you right now and taking you inside? How's he going to feel when his number one investigator has just got picked up, stuck in a cell, sitting having conversations with me?'

'He knows I wouldn't speak,' said the man.

'Lord Argyle doesn't know those sorts of things,' said Clarissa. 'He just ensures he doesn't have to, and with what he's after this time, it's not going to be a good couple of uppercuts in the jail. He'll take you out. You know that, don't you?'

Diggory looked around him. 'Look, I got what he asked. I found the man and the woman he was looking for. I didn't have a name.'

'If you didn't have a name, how did you find them?' asked Macleod.

'He gave me photographs, said they were looking about on the circuit, talking to people, and they had. They'd been putting feelers out here, there, and everywhere about selling a major item.'

'Why didn't Lord Argyle simply go to them, offer them more money than anyone else if he knew something was in the market?'

The man looked around him again, his voice becoming croakier. Macleod was sure he was shivering. 'He thinks it's real.'

'Real?' said Clarissa. 'That's a bit of a jump. How do you mean real? Real medieval or real?'

'Real,' said the man.

Macleod coughed and put his hand up. 'For those of us not in the antiques world, can we stop speaking in code? What do you mean medieval or real?'

'It's like I said to you, Inspector. Think about what something like Aaron's Rod is. Do you believe it to be the actual staff that Aaron carried and the one that God transformed into a snake, or do you believe it to be the relic that appeared in medieval times?'

'The difference being?' asked Macleod.

'The difference being,' said Diggory, 'one is a lot of money to get into the right hands. You can sell it. It's a story. It's a load of bluff. The other, the real, is fuel for people looking for power.'

'They say the root of all evil is the love of money', said Clarissa. 'Well, it's what the Good Book says. I'm not sure I agree with that. The love of power probably outstrips money. It's just money sometimes is associated with it.'

'He can't seriously think it's real,' said Macleod, but he

noticed that Diggory's face had gone white.

'He knows it's real. That's what he told me. Of course, I didn't say that to anybody else, but he said to me, "We need that at all costs." He said he would pay me extravagantly for it as well, but I turned him down. I said I'd just do my job under standard rates. He knows I didn't believe, but he put a tail on me.'

'Because he didn't trust you,' said Macleod.

'Maybe, but there was other people involved when he put the bid in.'

'He put the bid in?' asked Clarissa. 'That was him online?'

'Well, not him,' said Diggory, 'one of his people. When they knew this Rod was coming up at the auction house, they put a bid in and then the internet went dead. The next thing, it's been sold, so of course, he gets a hold of people that had been at the auction. They talk about this couple, the ones who bought it, and he says to me, "Find them," so I did. I said, "Do you want me to acquire the said item back?" I was happy to pay them. Nothing funny, Inspector, before that look in your face gets serious. I don't do that. Clarissa will tell you. I sort things out, make deals. I don't rough people up.'

Macleod saw Clarissa nod. 'But he didn't want you to,' said the Inspector.

'No. He told me to walk clear once I'd found him. In fact, I've kept my nose clean until coming here, and I only came because it was you, Cara, or should I say, Clarissa?'

'You should most definitely say Clarissa, Detective Sergeant Urquhart, if you will. Well, Diggory, thank you for the information. We shall discreetly depart and not bother you. Don't worry. We won't tell anybody where this information has come from.'

'You better not,' said the man. Macleod noticed that his face was white, and his hands were shaking. Diggory stood up, and this time walked away not in a dishevelled fashion but in a nervous one, looking over his shoulder this way and that, almost breaking into a half run as he disappeared out to a long path around the corner of a hedge.

'How far is it to his car?' asked Macleod.

'Oh, maybe a hundred yards or so.'

'Come on,' said Macleod, and stood up.

'What?' asked Clarissa.

'That man is as nervous as anything. He's leaving here expecting something. You can tell. You can tell the shoulder's nervous, but with almost an acceptance that something's going to happen.'

'Really, Inspector,' said Clarissa. 'I think that's a bit of an overreaction.' Before she could finish her sentence, Macleod was already running ahead, having seen Diggory disappear behind the hedge. Clarissa followed. When she caught up with the Inspector, he was standing at the edge of the carpark watching Diggory's car disappear. There was steep incline up to the car park, and Macleod saw the man speed up arriving at it, taking it at far too great a pace. He was obviously nervous and in a panic.

'See,' said Clarissa, 'nothing to—'

A gunshot rang out. Macleod saw the tire of Diggory's car half explode. The next second, the car turned, and was impaled into a wall at the bottom of a hill.

'Come on,' shouted Macleod.

'That's gunfire. Get cover,' said Clarissa.

'The man's in the line of fire,' said Macleod. 'Come on, we need to get him out of there.'

Macleod's eyes raced left and right, running behind cars in the car park, trying to give any shooter as little a sight of him as possible. When he reached the top of the hill, he realized it was open ground all the way down to where the car hit the wall. Without stopping, he quickly ran down the hill, sliding in behind the car and pulling open the door on the far side, away from where the shooter had been. Inside, he saw the airbag had exploded and Diggory was lying bent over.

'Are they out there? Are they out there?'

Macleod peered out through the window, searching the grounds around him. Clarissa arrived slightly out of breath and crouched down low behind the car as well.

'Can you see anything?' asked Macleod. 'Pop your head up quickly to see if there's anyone there.'

'No,' said Clarissa, 'I can't see anything' With that, Macleod decided to pull Diggory out through the door on his side.

'Get backups,' said Macleod. 'Quick. We have a shooter out there.' The Inspector made his way around to the front of the car, moving quickly in behind some trees beyond the wall. As he ran along, he saw a figure in the distance and then heard a car. He watched it pull up. Somebody got in, and the car drove away.

Black, he thought. *Hatchback*, but he couldn't see any number plate. Macleod had lost them and he looked back at the wall with the car crashed into it. *This has been a warning*, he thought. *You don't take a shot like that, disable a car, and then not come over and finish off the job. In fact, if they were such a good shot to hit the tire, why wouldn't they have just taken his head off? Yes, this was a warning. Argyle was certainly tracing his man.*

Chapter 15

Ross looked at the house before him, one of so many grey buildings on the estate. It was a chipped stone, weathered appearance, bland in itself for a building that contained four flats. In the front garden was a supermarket trolley upturned with a wheel missing, and Ross saw four satellite dishes attached to the outside wall of the house, presumably one for each flat.

On the street was a red Mondeo, its right wheel missing, and the car supported on bricks. As he began to walk up towards the front door of the leftmost flat, Ross saw a horde of kids marching down the street, laughing away and pointing at something, mocking it. He felt out of place in his suit and almost had an urge to undo his tie, but he was a detective and whoever answered the door would need to understand that. Alastair Hughes was on the Facebook page of Howie Lemmon, and although there were not many who seemed to use the forum to communicate with Howie, Alastair was one of them. From his image on Facebook, Alistair was a ginger-haired man with a freckly face, but as for his build, there were no pictures available that gave a glimpse into what lay beyond the man's shoulders.

Ross pressed the doorbell and, on hearing no sound, rapped

the door with his fist. There was a shout from somewhere and then silence. Ross waited twenty seconds, and then he rapped again with his fist.

'Go away. I've told you kids before, just go away. Piss off.' Ross rapped the door again.

'It's not the kids, Mr. Hughes.' Ross waited another moment, then he heard someone moaning. A man got up, came to the front door, and as it clicked back, Ross was taken aback by the figure in the fine old dressing gown with a pair of white Y-fronts. Clearly, the man wasn't bothered about being seen like this and he stood on the front door, one arm up against the frame, and gave Ross a belligerent stare.

'Who the hell are you?'

'Detective Constable Ross, sir. I'm looking for a Howie Lemmon. I believe he may be in danger. You were a contact on Facebook. I was wondering if you knew where Mr. Lemmon lived.'

'Is he in trouble?'

'Not with us, sir. He may be with other people, and I need to get to him. Are you aware of where he lives?'

'Well, you've seen him on Facebook. Why don't you just befriend him? Ask him where he lives.' This was a good point and needed refuting.

'The trouble Howie is in, he may not realize that we are his best option. Therefore, he may run.'

'You want me to snitch Howie in on you?'

'No,' said Ross, 'it's not like that at all. I want you to protect Howie. I want you to allow us to make sure he's safe.'

The man laughed, reached across under one armpit, scratching it. He broke wind, giving a little giggle as he did so, and then looked at the kids walking past on the street. They jeered at him, and he gave them two fingers in response. 'Pesky little brats. Somebody should take a strap to them. What do you say, officer?'

Ross was getting impatient. 'I would say you answer my question, or we can go and answer it somewhere else. Do you know where Howie Lemmon lives?' The man was almost affronted, and Ross found it difficult not to be snickering behind his policeman's face.

'Okay, easy. There's no need for that sort of thing. Howie's just around two streets away, Almond Avenue. He's number six. He'd be up the top floor. It's one of the nice, salubrious apartments like my own.'

Ross could see the man had humour but he smelt like a dead kipper. 'Thank you for your time, sir. Do you know if Howie's in at the moment?'

'Howie, I have seen about once in the last year. We talk occasionally on Facebook and then he's off doing his thing. He's found some stick. Metal detecting, that's Howie, digging up things. Did you know he dug up the football pitch? Just went around in the middle of the night, dug up the football pitch. He'd the team round. He's no friend of mine, I just happen to know him. If any of these other people who you seem to think want to do Howie some harm come, you make sure they understand. I'm an acquaintance, just somebody who knows him. Nothing more, nothing less.'

'If any of those people come round to ask me questions,' said Ross, 'they'd probably end up in a cell and, secondly, I don't give out information about other people. We have your confidentiality to look after.'

'Good to hear it,' said the man. 'Go. Go on then. Fight the good fight.' Ross turned away, but the image of the white Yfront's and the white hairy belly hanging over them was not fleeing from his mind as quickly as he wanted. He jumped into his car and drove the two streets round, finding Howie Lemmon's flat. There was a woman on the small lawn outside. She seemed to be planting what Ross thought were begonias but, in truth, it could have been any type of flower. He wasn't that accurate, unlike his partner.

'Excuse me, ma'am,' said Ross and saw the woman look up. She had grey hair tied back and a face that had seen many years. She pushed the glasses she had back up her nose, but they were only half-rims, and she still seemed to be looking over the top of them. Ross wondered, was this just the force of habit. He remembered somebody else he worked with closely who did that.

'Are you a salesman?'

Ross was a little taken aback. 'No, I'm looking for Howie Lemmon.'

'You look like a salesman with that suit. A car like that is a bit expensive for around here. Awfully expensive for any of Howie's friends.'

'I'm DC Ross, ma'am. I'm looking for a Howie Lemmon in connection with an incident I'm working on. Would Howie be at home?'

'Possibly,' said the woman. 'He's incredibly quiet, Howie. Sometimes, he doesn't seem to come out of that flat for a week. He's a good neighbour to have though. He doesn't say anything, he doesn't do anything. In fact, the only time he does something is usually in the middle of the night, and it's not around here. He's off digging up or "detectoring", as he calls it. Yes, I think he's still upstairs,' she said.

'Thank you,' said Ross, and marched over to the second front door on the ground level on the left-hand side of the grey building. Again, he tried the bell but on hearing no response, he rapped the door, and then he rapped it a second time. He rapped it a third and a fourth, but again there was no reply. Ross made his way back to the woman in the garden.

'Are you sure he's in?' asked Ross.

'Well, he went in last Monday. I'm sure of that. I thought I heard somebody a day or two after that, but I'm not sure. My hearing is not that good. I'm old, you see. It's what happens. It'll happen to you, too.' Ross tried not to take that personally. 'He certainly hasn't come out since then unless he came out in the middle of the night. Can you see anything at the windows?'

'No. Why?' asked Ross.

'Because Howie will be looking. Usually, he wouldn't answer the door but if you rapped it, he'd be up at that window looking down, nosing to see who it was. He was very suspicious, suspicious of everybody. He thought I was put here by MI5 to look after him. I mean, look at me. It's the greatest cover story ever.' Ross tried not to laugh, instead, giving a smile that he had perfected over the years. 'Right next door, the guy's a painter; he might have a set of ladders you could borrow. I think he's still there. Is that—? Yes, that looks like his van on the drive. If you go and see him, he might have some ladders and you could look in the window. See if you're having to break the door down.'

Ross thanked the woman. He reckoned this could be a good idea and took a quick scan of the upstairs windows and realized they were not covered, curtains drawn back.

It took Ross about five minutes to negotiate with the painter next door, and the man helped him bring around a long ladder and put it up to the windows. Ross thought he looked rather bizarre, clambering up in his grey suit, jacket flapping in a light breeze as he reached the top.

Looking in the first window, he could see a kitchen. It was a small unit, but what interested him the most was that on the side, there were two sandwiches, butter spread on them, and what looked like some chicken sitting beside it. It was hard to tell the colour of things through that window with the lack of light coming from inside the building.

'Have you seen enough, mate?' It was the painter from down below.

'We'll need to check another window. I can't see anything in there. Just worried in case he's fallen or something.' Ross saw the man give a nod, but his body language said, "Hurry up. I've got things to do." Ross made his way down, and he adjusted the ladder round to the rear window. Ross again climbed up, and this time saw a bedroom with an open door behind it. The bedroom was a mess, covers lying here, there, and everywhere, some cheap CDs kicking about, but Ross wasn't interested. What had caught his attention was through the open door. He saw what looked like the bottom end of a bath, but just inside the view of the door, he thought he saw a leg with a socked foot at the bottom of it. It was perfectly still, not moving at all.

Ross climbed quickly down the ladder.

'You got anything to force the door?' asked Ross.

The man looked at him. 'Force the door? Why? What's the matter?'

'Have you got anything to force the door?'

'I have a sledgehammer I use sometimes for work.'

'Get it,' said Ross. 'Get it now.'

Ross didn't wait for the arrival of the sledgehammer. Instead, he tried putting his shoulder to the door. The old woman from the garden had made her way around, seeing the agitation of the man.

'What's up, Mr. Policeman? What's up?'

'Just stay back,' said Ross. 'I need to get up there.'

'Is Howie all right? I mean, he was always a funny lad, but is he okay?'

Ross didn't answer. The painter from next door arrived holding a sledgehammer. Ross took it, smacking the lock several times before the door flew back, opening. Dropping the sledgehammer, Ross ran up the tight stairways across orange carpet that may even have come from the seventies. As he reached the top of the steps, he tried to orientate himself, but instead, just looked in every door. When he saw the bedroom, he turned around one hundred and eighty degrees and almost walked into the leg of Howie Lemmon. His automatic instinct was to reach out and grab the pair of hanging legs to hold the man upright. But as he did so, he could feel the body was cold, lifeless, and limp, and he looked straight up into eyes that had no life in them.

'Is he there? Is he there?'

Ross stepped back hearing the old woman's voice and realized that she was close.

'Just stay back. Just stay back.'

'Why? What's the matter? Where's Howie?' Ross moved back out of the bathroom and the woman ran into him in the small hallway. Behind her was the painter.

'Do you need help?'

'No,' said Ross. 'I need everybody to just go back down the steps and stand outside. I'm afraid there's nothing can be done for Howie now.' With that, the woman looked around the corner of the bathroom. Ross saw her shoulders begin to shake. Her hands flew to her face, and she began to cry and she collapsed suddenly on the floor.

Ross grabbed his mobile, dialled 999, advised the operator who he was, and requested an immediate ambulance to his location, as well as that the murder team in Inverness be advised. The painter was over with the old woman, checking her airways and breathing.

'I think she's just out cold,' he said. 'I've done my first aid. She's just cold. We need to get something under her head, put her in the right position, make sure she's okay.' Ross nodded and encouraged the man, and then turned to look back inside the bathroom. There was no way Howie put himself up there. Inside, Ross cursed, another lead gone, somebody else who could explain what was happening.

Chapter 16

Macleod was back at the Inverness station, sitting in his chair behind his desk. He had just finished a large amount of paperwork and was about to start working through some mail that had arrived during the day. Yesterday, Ross had discovered Howie Lemmon around about the same time as Macleod was hunting a shooter. But thankfully since then, things had been routine. Not that they couldn't have got more out of hand. After all, he had three dead bodies now and someone shot at but, in truth, not many leads.

Clarissa had headed back to the station to try and work out why. She was also still working contacts to see if anyone knew about the Rod being sold on. But in truth, she was finding that everyone had suddenly gone quiet. Who could blame them? They've just seen somebody shot at, with at least two dead bodies now in the papers. Howie Lemmon was about to become public.

Whenever an investigation stalled like this, Macleod always thought you should put out every feeler you could. He started calling other agencies including a call to the Coastguard advising them that there may be an expensive art item leaving the country and one of the possible routes for that, of course, was on a boat. Easier to smuggle away than trying to take it through any airport. He also advised many of the airports in Scotland as he thought the best thing to do was make as many people aware as possible. Photographs of Aaron's Rod were circulated and anything untoward was asked to be noted to him.

His conversation with a DCI that morning had not gone well. That was always the case of people higher up wanting things done immediately. It took Macleod a good half an hour of explanation to point out what they had done before the man got off his back. That was the joy of leading the team. He'd rather have handed him over to Hope or something, because the man liked Hope and who wouldn't? Be it a man or woman, you'd rather talk to this lively Glasgow woman than Mardy Macleod, as he once been known. The DCI probably would have got more out of Hope as well. Macleod was well known for keeping his cards within his own hand and not sharing them too high above. That stopped them coming up with any stupid ideas and sending you off on wild goose chases. But at the moment, most things seem like a wild goose chase.

He left the letters from the post at the front of his desk, and stood up, before taking a short walk out of his office to get himself some coffee. He looked over to where Ross usually was, but the man was absent as he had gone over to help Jona at Howie Lemon's house. Hope was shortly to join him. Macleod made his way over to her once he had picked up his coffee.

'Do you want one yourself?' asked Macleod.

'No, it's fine. I'm just going back over the statements making sure we haven't missed anything. I think we have a handle on what's going on. We just don't have a handle on who's doing it. There's definitely two parties looking for this Rod, isn't there?'

'So it would seem, and if we don't get to it first, I think we could end up seeing one destroy the other, or vice versa. I've put the feelers out, spread the net as far as I can. We've still got some stop and search going on as well.'

'Yes, I was reading some of the reports back from that,' said Hope. 'There's nothing there either. Is Clarissa not coming up with anything in the art world?'

'She says it's all closed down. Nobody's speaking, and no wonder—people are dying out there. People shot at. It's a good way to make sure people stay quiet.'

'You don't usually get a lot of guns used in this country. Armed robberies, yes, but pot shots like this seem rather strange,' said Hope.

'I don't think these people are used to working in the light too much. It's very public. If there is some sort of secret society, some sort of religious nut fest going on,' said Macleod, 'they usually keep themselves in the dark. It's better to coerce from the darkness than it is to try and force something in the light.'

'I'll see what Ross turns up from Harry's flat. I'm going back there in about half an hour to see him.'

'Very good,' said Macleod. 'You okay?'

'Yes, why?'

'Clarissa, she's coming in at your level, but she's working very close with me. You know it's not a slur, don't you? She's not coming in at number two. You're number two, that's why you're with Ross. Clarissa's under supervision. She might be a sergeant, but she's coming from a vastly different world. So, I'm just keeping an eye. Once we get through this case, we'll be back to the old times—you, me, and whoever else underneath.'

Hope smiled and looked up at him. 'You're getting overly sweet in your old age. Do you know that? Thinking about my feelings. There was a time when you just told me what to do.'

'I'm just aware I can sometimes take you for granted, Hope. Sometimes, I just charge on expecting people around me to just do what they're told when they're told it.'

'I'd never put you down as a touchy, feely boss. But no, Seoras, I'm fine. Let's get back to work.'

Macleod took his coffee and made his way back to the office, plonking himself down in his chair again and opening up the letters before him. There were a few requests for information, some other bits, and old cases, points to be clarified, things that could be put aside for another day.

At the bottom of the pile was an elegant letter. The envelope itself spoke of class and the address in the front was written in script, in the calligraphy style. Macleod thought it looked like it should be on a wedding album, not in the front of a letter to a policeman. He ran his thumb on the inside of the envelope, breaking the paper at the top of the envelope and taking out a piece of parchment inside. Again, it was no hum-drum letter, but a very delicately written item. Macleod laid back in his chair, held the letter before him, and read the very first line.

'The Order of St. Columbus Knights, guardians of all things of the Holy.'

Macleod looked up. There were times in the murder squad that people could be humorous, and with what was going on, this letter felt like some sort of prank. But the writing was too good; everything about it was too clever.

'To Detective Inspector Seoras Macleod.'

To him personally, there was a threat in that. It wasn't just simply to a man in charge of an investigation. They were letting him know that he was identified.

'We respectively ask for the cessation of all activities towards the recovery of Aaron's Rod. It shall be placed into the hands of those who the Highest and Holiest requires to perform His work. Any other activity will be seen as an act against the Almighty. Please advise your fellow foot soldiers, Sergeant Hope McGrath, Sergeant Clarissa Urquhart, and DC Alan Ross. We would hate for anything to happen to them or to you, or indeed to any of your families regardless of how they see God's own law. You have been warned. Yours,'

Macleod stared at the signature, there were two, Alpha and the second one was Omega. The blood began to rise in Macleod, he knew his Bible well. God described Himself as Alpha and Omega, and for somebody else to take those names angered him. He'd also been threatened, not just him, but Jane, his partner, and they had threatened the team as well. That, Macleod was used to, that could happen. They had all signed up to it, but not the families. Not Ross's partner, not Hope's new boyfriend, and he would have to ask Clarissa who her family were.

'Hope,' shouted Macleod, through the closed door, 'need you now.'

He looked down at the letter, leaving it on his desk. The red head of Hope opened the door, quizzically, but she then entered fully when she saw Macleod's sullen face.

'What's the matter Seoras?'

'We've just been sent a threatening letter. Come around. Look at it.'

'That's fancy,' said Hope, and began to read it.

'Alpha, Omega,' said Macleod.

'And?' said Hope.

'They signed it with God's name. I am the Alpha and Omega.'

'It seems nuts. You think this is genuine?'

'The bullets shot the other day, they certainly felt genuine. I

137

think somebody shot a very genuine bullet at you.'

'If they're from the same place.'

'Well, they both don't have the Rod wherever they were from,' said Macleod.

'You taking this seriously?' said Hope pointing at the letter. Macleod nodded. 'Do you want me to get uniform involved? Set up some protection?'

'Completely. You need to get on to Clarissa though. I'm not sure yet who her family is, where they are. I'm just going to put a quick call to Jane. I think she needs to take a little stay somewhere else.'

'Good idea,' said Hope, 'I'll get onto it right away,' and with that, she marched over to the door.

'Oh, Hope. The boyfriend.'

'Do you think they know him?'

'They called us all by name in here. No risks. You need to talk to him. You need to set something up for him. If he can take a short holiday all the better. You know the drill.'

Macleod saw Hope's face fall. 'I was hoping to keep him out of this,' she said.

'We all do; remember what happened to Jane though?' Hope reached up and touched her face. The scar that ran across her cheek she'd obtained saving Macleod's partner from an acid bath in their house.

'Good point sir. I'll get right on it.

And with that she was gone. Macleod stood up and stared out the window. He could feel the blood rising. In his day, he'd been a heavily religious man. Now, he liked to think of himself as less religious, but more a man of faith. Some of the older determined convictions have gone. Marriage before sex. Attitudes towards those of a different lifestyle. That was how they put it. That had changed. He was much more relaxed. But these people were using God. Those who would abuse God, his attitude to them had probably got stronger, more determined.

He wanted to pick up the letter, rip it apart, find someone and shove it down their throat, but he knew he had to leave it to get it examined. In his heart, he hoped that it would bring something to the investigation, a slip-up, but his head said that this was done well. It would have been posted in a random post box in the middle of nowhere, no CCTV.

Did these people seriously believe that this staff, this Rod of Aaron would be used by God to do what? In the Bible, in the story, it was being used to suppress someone who was harming God's people. What did these people think they were going to do with it? In his own head, he'd been struggling of late. How much of the faith was myth? True, but not historically true. How much of it was real to him? He knew God was. But with things like this, he was no longer of such a sound mind. Back home in Lewis a lot of them would've said he'd gone off the rails, lost his faith. Macleod believed he'd found it. He believed nowadays he could take on the questions. He could live with doubt. But this, acts of people like this still incensed him as they claimed to be people of God when they murdered to get what they wanted. He looked down at his fist and it was clenched tight, his fingers red. Macleod took a deep breath, reached for his mobile phone, pressed the image of Jane, his partner. Someone had come for her once and they certainly wouldn't be doing it again.

Chapter 17

Ross was standing on the driveway at the side of the small grey building he had been in the previous day. The older woman who had collapsed at seeing the body of Howie Lemmon had recovered and was now pottering around outside her house, watching the investigation going on. Earlier, she had brought up a cup of tea to Ross, trying to extract information about what was being found inside, but Ross was experienced enough to keep everything pleasant without giving any real information away. Having handed the empty cup back to her, he was awaiting Jona to come and see him. The lead forensic investigator had made a discovery and just was trying to clear the way for Ross to come in. She'd said there were a few other things they needed to check, so rather than contaminate the scene with Ross, she decided to get that done first and then invite him along. Ross had dressed in white coveralls and now he was waiting.

It hadn't been the first body Ross had seen, but as with any, they did affect you. It wasn't the image when he arrived and gone into the bathroom, but rather that half a leg that he'd seen from the top of the ladder. What had made it colder was Macleod's phone call and then briefing later that day in the office. Someone was threatening them, but not just them, not just the team. They were threatening their families. Ross thought of his partner at home. The man was proud of Ross, proud of what he had done in climbing the ranks as a detective. He had always been supportive in those bad days when Ross had gone home, struggling with what he'd seen. A mild-mannered Ross grew angry at the thought that someone would come after a lover he considered to be gentle and only ever supportive.

'Ready for you,' shouted Jona from the front door of the flat. Ross skipped his way over, pulling up the hood of the white coverall and followed Jona up the stairs towards the back bedroom.

'There was a floorboard over here that just didn't seem right, creaking all the time, close to the edge in a place where there was only one small item of furniture. This table, Ross, and you can move it without even thinking about it, very little on it. As far as making himself a hidey-hole, the guy really didn't think too much about it,' said Jona.

'No, I can see that, not the cleverest. I guess you were onto it right away.'

Jona turned round and smiled at him. 'We did find something inside it though,' and she led Ross over to the bed, on which lay some plastic sheeting, atop of which was an A5 red book. Ross donned his gloves and carefully opened up the front of it. There was no detail on it, but simply a number of addresses within.

'Nothing with it at all?' asked Ross.

'No,' said Jona, 'absolutely nothing.'

'I took a scan over it,' said Jona, 'but I don't recognize any of them.'

Ross' finger traced down the different addresses. 'I take it you're going to want to keep hold of the book. I'm going to have to take a manual copy of this.'

'I'll get the photographer in. We'll do you a nice one of the list. You can take that and go.'

'You find anything else untoward?'

'Not really,' said Jona. 'He's got a small library section. You go and have a look at it.' Together, they left and went into the lounge area in the front of the flat. There was a small sofa, a large TV, and several metal detectors stuffed into the corner. On one wall was a small shelf with a number of books on detectoring, but also different antiques. Ross took the books off the shelf and started flicking through the antique literature. As he spun through one in particular, a piece of paper flew out from an open page, and Ross held the book at that point. He scanned around, realizing he was on a page of ancient artifacts.

The title at the top was *The Weapons of God*, which seemed rather aggressive to Ross, and he looked down seeing a picture of the Ark of the Covenant. There were other items, swords and things, but Ross just wasn't sure what some of them had to do with the Creator, but he saw that a small paragraph on Aaron's Rod was highlighted. Beneath it was a picture of an old man and a snake in front of him, half gobbling up other snakes, in front of a group of other old men.

'It seems he knew about the myth. Anyway,' said Jona, 'does that make any sense to you?'

'It doesn't make sense to me if he thinks this is Aaron's Rod. I mean, it would be worth a fortune, but then maybe he doesn't know what it is. Maybe he's found something.'

'Was there any metal in the rod?' asked Jona. 'It's just, he's a metal detectorist. I thought a rod from that time would have had wood, jewels on it maybe, but it's more likely been a staff, isn't it?'

'Clarissa reckons it's not from that time. It's from the Middle Ages. Reckons it was put together, so it may have had metal in it. She said that's more important than the actual physical item. That's where the price comes from.'

Jona nodded. 'Well, it's not hidden in here anyway, in this flat. Howie Lemmon didn't have it. He may have had it at one point, but it's not here now. But whoever killed did a search, but not a good one.'

'Anything else you can say about Howie?'

'Well, the suicide, it's all staged. He's hung up there like he's affixed on a tie up to the ceiling. You can see the small fan and the knot that was around it. There's no chair. There's nothing. I mean, it's actually a really amateur effort of making it look like suicide.'

'Unless they didn't want people to know. Maybe they wanted them to think he was killed deliberately.'

'Holding it like a threat?' asked Jona.

'Exactly,' said Ross. 'There seems to be a lot of threats going around at the moment.'

'He was definitely dead beforehand, but he was asphyxiated. Professionally done, too. Arm around from the back. He's gone completely then they hang him up.' Ross felt a chill down his spine, coming from all the threats that were going about. His mind wandered again to his partner and to the image of Howie Lemmon hanging from the ceiling.

'You okay?' asked Jona.

'Not really. You know they made a threat, don't you, against the team?'

'Yes,' said Jona. 'It's nothing unusual, is it?'

'They threatened our families as well. Macleod reckons

143

they're right nutters, zealots capable of doing it. He's organized protection.'

'Well, I can see why that would be bothering you. Best get it closed quick then.'

'Yes,' said Ross with a sigh. He had hoped Jona would have something more inspirational, something more comforting, but the woman knew the score too well and wasn't ready to do that.

Taking his leave of Jona, Ross made his way back to his car, taking off his coverall, and drove into town. The photographer had taken a picture of the addresses in the book and emailed them to Ross's account, and he began a trawl throughout the afternoon of the various locations.

Many seemed to be cafés and pubs, places where people would meet, but none of them were named as such. They all had the street number rather than the actual title of the property. Ross drove from the west to the east side of Inverness and to the north and the south, crisscrossing the town, each time coming to places that didn't seem to have anything to do with antiques. Each time he stepped inside, asked the landlord or the person running the café if they knew of a Howie Lemmon, but all came back negative.

Why would anyone hold addresses? thought Ross. He then found an address that was right in the middle of Inverness city centre. Driving to it, he found it to be on the third floor of one of the older buildings, just off the main road. Ross loved the height that the city centre had. You could stand and look up at floors, see the old grey buildings looking back at you, giving the town a sense of history. It was a sharp contrast to the many new estates with the modern bright houses. This was proper building, back in a time when it would have taken many men maybe a year or two to construct some of these. There was architecture at the top as well, occasional gargoyles and other little designs that were missed by the people marching along the street on their daily trips to work.

Ross found his building and hiked up the three flights of stairs to the top. As he reached the door, he saw the 'For Rent' sign on it. It was locked, and he checked the hiring company's name on the front, making a note before googling them on his phone. They were just around the corner, so he traipsed all the way back along the street and found the offices of MacNair's.

The office was bright and swish, and at the front desk, Ross saw a young girl who smiled at him, and then looked a little bit bemused when Ross held his warrant card.

'I need to find who's renting the office on the street around the corner. Can you do that for me?'

The girl seemed panicked and then offered Ross a cup of tea while she went to get the boss. Ross declined and sat patiently until two minutes later, an older man arrived, sweeping back his hair.

'Hi, I'm Alan, Alan Greenwood. I'm running MacNair's at the moment. Is there a problem?'

'No, there isn't,' said Ross. 'I'm just following through some investigations, and I need to know who's hired that building around the corner.'

The man smiled. 'Certainly. Just give me the details. Let's go over here to this computer.' Ross stood behind the nervous man who typed away on the keyboard as Ross gave the address. Making a note of it on his phone, Ross thanked the man and then began to google the address to see where in Inverness he was going. When he came up with no results, Ross turned back to the owner.

'Just check that name again for me, would you?' The man pulled up the record, and it was as Ross had seen. 'Do you mind if I stay here and use your computer for a minute? Because that address isn't coming up.' The man looked too nervous to refuse and took Ross into a back room, plonking him in front of another computer. 'Please feel free to do whatever you need. Is there something wrong?'

'There is because that address is not coming up. I'm not sure it is an address in this city. How long was the office hired for?'

'Well, the minimum rent, officer, was at least two weeks. We said that to the man at the time. He was quite insistent he wanted to hire it by the hour. We don't do that, but we hired it for two weeks. It was really the least we could do. I did also say to him there are other places who will rent you rooms. A lot of the service stations and hotels have side rooms and the hotels would do you a room for a while, but he declined them all.'

'Why would he do that?' asked Ross.

'Well, the man seemed quite paranoid. I took him up to the office. He was checking the windows, looking down all the time.'

Something resonated with Ross, and he took out his mobile phone, holding it in front of him. He described the features of Howie Lemmon to the man. The bushy eyebrows, slightly squint left side of the jaw, and the crazy hair.

'That's him,' said the man.

'What was he wearing?' asked Ross.

'Well, it was like a—oh, you know those camo jackets? You know, you can pick them up at army surplus stores, things like that.'

That sounds promising, thought Ross. He made a call to Jona to check the wardrobe. There was an army camo jacket.

'I'm going to show you something, sir, and I'll need you to not to repeat this to anybody else or talk about it. Unfortunately, I don't have a photograph of the man alive. I only have one of him dead. I'd like you to identify him if you could.'

The man gave a start. 'Do I really need to?'

'It will help, sir. Just to clarify for me what's going on here.'

Ross turned the phone around and the man took a quick look. 'Please do make sure it is him.'

The owner continued to stare, and then he turned away quite shaken and took a long drink. 'That's him, all right. That's him.'

'Sorry to put you through that. Did he pay his bill?'

'In advance in cash, and the name he gave me was Jeremy, Jeremy Matthews.

'Thank you for your time. I think you've helped me realize something.' With that, Ross took his leave of the estate agent and made his way back to his car, where he placed a call to Macleod.

'Ross, Jona said you had something. She said you're off checking addresses. Tell me you've got good news because we're struggling this end.'

'Sorry, but I don't, sir. We discovered a book in Howie's secret hidey-hole with a load of addresses and I've checked them all out. Most are just normal pubs and clubs, nothing untoward about them. One, however, was a rented office which Howie Lemmon rented under a false name. He wanted it for a sharp, quick meeting, but he had to rent it for two weeks. When told this, he didn't go elsewhere, he wanted that room. Now, it's at a height and it looks down on the street. Howie also knew about Aaron's Rod. Whether or not he knew the item he had was Aaron's Rod is another matter, but he was aware what the myth was. I believe he was hiring the room to check it out. Unfortunately, it would only just be him and probably Forrest Mackenzie. I'll get on the CCTV from the building and see if I can confirm that, but I reckon Forrest Mackenzie met him there.'

'If the man only knows about the myth and isn't able to identify what he's got, Forrest Mackenzie could tell him a whopper and take it and run. Forrest Mackenzie wouldn't be looking from a ten percent cut. He'd be looking to sell it on the cheap to somebody who actually works for him and then shift the thing on for real. This is starting to make sense, Ross. Unfortunately, it isn't getting us any closer to who has the Rod now or who's after it.'

Chapter 18

Macleod was impatient the day was not going well, Ross had phoned saying he had gone through everything, all the addresses on the list, and had come up with nothing other than a confirmed meeting between Forrest Mackenzie and Howie Lemon. It appeared that Howie Lemon had found Aaron's Rod or whatever the item actually really was and had gone to Forrest Mackenzie. From there, the item had been put on sale at a greatly reduced price. It seemed that Howie was being duped by the man but someone had taken a tail to Howie. Whoever was looking for the item now was not afraid to dispatch the bodies, so nothing would get traced back to them.

Of course, Macleod was still confused. There were two parties interested, one he believed to be Argyle's group, but were they the Order of St. Columbus Knights? Macleod was unsure. Were there two religious groups after this? His dinner in the canteen of the Inverness police station had passed into his mouth, but in truth, he couldn't tell you what he had eaten. This was not to do with the quality of the food, but rather his absent-mindedness from eating. Instead, his every thought was about the case, including the welfare of Jane, his partner.

He had phoned her twice already today and now she was on the road, off to stay under a pseudonym at a hotel. She had a friend with her, so she was posing as being on a girls' weekend, but Jane was well aware of why she was going.

Sitting at his desk, Macleod was poring back over the statements and all the evidence so far collected. Was he missing something? Because at the moment, there was nowhere to go. He was in that situation of waiting for something to happen, waiting for a lead to fall, something to come to him. He had done the spadework; he had put out feelers to other agencies. He had made sure people were aware of what he was looking for, but it still didn't make it any easier waiting.

When the telephone rang, Macleod took three rings to answer it; his mind was fixated on Lord Argyle, a man he barely knew but he was deciding he might need to get to know sooner rather than later.

'Macleod.'

'James Anderson, Inspector. We've got the Coast Guard on for you from Stornoway, the operations centre. They said that you'd put a feeler out and they may have some information for you."

'Put them through, James; thank you.'

Macleod could feel his skin beginning to tingle, a feeling he got often but one that was often a prelude to disappointment. Anytime information was being given, Macleod was all ears, but so much of it was nothing.

'Hello, this is Inspector Seoras Macleod.'

'Hello, this is James from the coast guard at Stornoway.'

'Thank you for coming back to me. The sergeant said you might have something.'

'Yes. I don't know if it's anything but with the message

you put out, we thought best to let you decide that. There's a boat over in Lochinver, goes by the name of Sally's Tan. It's a motor cruiser and it's got a Cayman Island registration on it. Usually, it wouldn't cause any suspicion, but we received a phone call on the 999 line from a member of the public over in Lochinver saying someone had gone missing off the boat. We automatically thought it was someone in the water, so we started to send some teams and get hold of the vessel, but they told us that it wasn't the case; it was simply a guest they had who'd gone ashore and hadn't come back. We started trying to get some more details about where they had come from, where this guest was going and they were extremely obstructive in giving any information. Technically, for us, there's no reason to investigate any further, but I thought that you should know about it.'

'Did you ask specifically about the name of the guest?' asked Macleod.

'Yes. We didn't even get a first name, nothing at all.'

'Did they tell you where they had come from?'

'Negative, but we also traced the last passage of the boat—we're able to do that on the Automatic Identification System, except that they switched that off. They came out of Aberdeen on the way round.'

'Do you happen to know whereabouts the vessel is normally located.'

'We did have a look over the last month and it's normally around Aberdeen. It looks like it specifically came over this way. The AIS has been on most of the time, it drops out occasionally and not always in areas where we would expect it to, but they have the facilities to switch that off on board.'

'You're saying at times they may be making a deliberate effort to not be seen.'

'It happens with fishermen; if you're in a good fishing area, you don't want everybody else ploughing in at the same time. They have a habit of knocking off their Automatic Identification, but a motor cruiser is unusual because why wouldn't they want someone to know when they're there?'

'Unless they are up to something nefarious. That's the implication, isn't it?' said Macleod.

'That's a bit of a step for us,' said James. 'As I said, there's nothing overly untoward for us, but we have to report on a person missing. They're not missing and are certainly not overdue. They're also on land. Technically, it's not our responsibility if they are missing.'

'You're saying that, actually, it becomes under our jurisdiction as a missing person, doesn't it, not on the coast, but on the land?'

'That would be correct,' said James.

'In that case, I might just send someone up to find out some more information, James. That's great.'

'Well, I hope that was helpful,' said James. 'As I said, we're not taking any other action, but if you need anything from us, please let us know.'

'Thank you,' said Macleod, 'really thank you.' He could feel the hairs in the back of his neck. Sometimes you had a gut feeling about something. As he sat back in the seat to think, the office door was knocked and was opened to reveal purple hair.

'Apologies, Seoras. I just wanted to come and say, there's not much point me being here anymore. I've exhausted most of my leads. People are not talking in the art world. They're a little bit shaken, too many people dead. We're talking about people who are genuinely here to make money out of a love of antiques. On the good side, they want to stay far away from it all. On the bad side, they can't provide any information because of that.'

'It's fine,' said Macleod, 'Come in and sit down.'

Clarissa stared at him a little bit surprised, but she made her way over and sat on the seat in front of Macleod's desk. 'What's up?' she asked. 'You've got that look on your face. Something's ticking in that brain, isn't it?'

'You know when you get something, a little bit of information, and it's really nothing. Something you just think, "Well, maybe, I'll send a uniform over."'

'Somebody's just given you one of these. Why haven't you left the room?' asked Clarissa.

'When you get up the ranks, and you're the head of a case like this, especially murder, you don't just charge out. If I went to this, and it's on the west side, all the way over in Lochinver, and it turned out to be nothing while things go off back here, it wouldn't reflect very well.'

'Lochinver,' queried Clarissa, 'But Lochinver's around the corner from Inchnadamph.'

'It is indeed,' said Macleod and he began to relay what the coast guard had said to him.

'So, you've got a missing person who's not missing? Well, really not missing, but on a boat that won't say anything about why they're there. I think we should ask the coast guard who owns the boat.'

'Well, that's a point,' said Macleod. 'They said it came out of Aberdeen, and I just naturally assumed.'

'It was Argyle's because he's over that direction.'

'Exactly.'

'Well, I think you're ahead of yourself there, Seoras. I'll give them a call. Find that where it is, see who owns it.'

'Better than that,' said Macleod, 'Go there. Go to Lochinver, find this boat, talk to the people.'

'Tonight?'

'Yes,' said Macleod, 'It might not be there tomorrow. It's only just gone six.'

'Okay, Seoras, if you think it's that good a lead.'

'It might be nothing,' said Macleod. 'It really might be, but I haven't been in this game this long to not spot the odd winner.'

Clarissa stood up. 'Should I take someone with me?'

'Do you need someone?' asked Macleod. 'It might look dodgy if you turn up with two people. If you bring uniform, they'd run a mile. If I was you, I'd keep a low profile while you find out your information.'

'Understood.'

'But,' said Macleod, 'if there's anything juicy, get back-up in straight away. Contact Hope or me direct. We'll be there quick as we can.'

It was eight o'clock when Clarissa arrived in Lochinver, driving into the small fishing town, which tonight was bathed in sunshine. There was still a stiff breeze blowing. So, when she got out of the car, she was glad she was wearing her jeans and not her skirt. She had changed knowing she was coming away from the office, but also was trying to look less like a detective. A long flowing pink scarf hung around her neck with a brown leather jacket over her shoulders. Her boots ran up to her knees, and while not the most practical, the heel wasn't too high, so she could still run. "Don't look like a police officer," Macleod had said. Well, she'd been doing that for most of her career.

Clarissa made her way over to a small shop and purchased an

ice cream before wandering along to the harbour side. She sat there, looking around, searching the boats. Alongside of the harbour you could see the coastguard orange boat looking all business in the summer sun. She was unable to locate Sally's Tan so Clarissa started to walk along the harbour until she saw a boat tied up to one side. A quick look at the motor cruiser allowed her to identify the vessel's name on the bow. She walked up with a camera and began taking photographs of it.

'What are you doing?' asked a voice.

'Sorry. Do you own this? Seriously, do you own this?'

'Why are you taking photographs?'

'Tom wants one of these,' said Clarissa. 'My Tom. He's down in Brighton at the moment, but he said to me, this is what he wants, one of these motor cruisers. I was walking along, looked at it, and I thought, "That's what Tom wants. That's the model. I'm sure of it." He showed me a photograph, I'm sure it looked the same as yours. He's talking about buying one. I said to him, "No, no way, we're not buying something until I've seen it properly."'

'And you saw it here?' queried the man.

'Yes. Sorry. I'm just on a bit of a holiday from some of the girls, they'll be going to dinner in about an hour or two. It's a late one, I fear we had a bit of a heavy afternoon. I was the designated driver so I'm here and sober. I thought I'd have a wander. Got an ice cream, but it's not proper, is it? You want one of the proper ice creams. That one's out of those machines, those Mr. Whippy things.'

The man was staring incoherently at Clarissa. She always found it best that if you didn't want somebody to ask awkward questions, you filled in the gaps.

'Tom says to me, "I found what we want, and this is it, this boat is it." Yours looks the same.'

'What make was it?'

'I don't know,' said Clarissa. 'I'm not the sailor, Tom is, but I wanted to see the interior. That's where I'm going to be, isn't it? He looks at it with a mariner's eye. He looks at all the communication stuff and all that safety stuff. Me, I don't care. I want to look at the rooms and see what sort of beds you have. Is it a decent shower? That's all I care. I couldn't give a toss about the other stuff. Would you mind? Would you mind if I pop down for ten minutes and have a look?'

'Have a look. You want to come on board?'

'Oh, are you at your dinner? Sorry, I could come back later. Don't worry if it's a mess, I don't care, I just need to see the fittings and that. You go abroad and he just packs next to nothing, then I have to pack everything for him, but then my stuff, I need plenty of space. You can understand that. A woman of my age to look classy, you don't walk around in a bikini, do you? You have to have a bit more style than that, you can't just get away with your looks anymore.'

The man laughed. Clarissa could tell he was starting to engage with her. 'You don't look so old. I think you have a bit of spirit.'

'Thank you. I hope Tom still thinks so. It's been a long marriage, twenty plus years. It's not easy.'

'I'm sure he's a lucky man.' With that, the man turned to go. Clarissa stared his back, his shoulders were broad, and you could tell he was used to heaving heavy weights about but he was dressed rather snappily—neat slacks with a smart top.

'I'm sorry, but would you mind really? Tom can be a bit, well impulsive. If I don't get a look at this, if I don't give him a reason why I don't want it, he's just going to buy it anyway, and that just kicks things off. I hate that.'

The man turned around. 'Why don't you just tell him to wait?'

'If your woman told you to wait, would you wait? No, you're a man of the sea like him, you would just do it. You guys, you make the decisions, you're the head, we're the neck, we point you in the right direction. That's how it works, isn't it?'

The man stepped to the edge of the boat, 'I guess there's no harm; it's not actually my boat. I just work on it.'

'Oh, sorry, do I need to talk to the owner?'

'No, you can't talk to the owner; he's not here,'

Clarissa thought about pushing the point asking who he was, but the man looked like he was going to let her get on board. She thought she should run with this, rather than pushing for who owned it.

'Well, I'll be as quick as I can,' said Clarissa. 'Seriously, in and out. Do you have somebody on board who's in charge that I will need to talk to, to sort of say thank you to.'

'No,' said the man, 'come on down, they've all gone off for something to eat; it's only me here.'

Clarissa realized what she was doing. She was about to go on board a boat with a man who she told had told she was on her own, and he was telling her to go down below where it would be just the two of them.

'Go on then,' she said. 'We'll have to be quick.' Clarissa took the hand of the man and stepped down onto the edge of the boat. He led her through the small cabin door into the heart of the cruiser. She looked around at the bridge, noting documents and papers sitting around, journey plans for where they were going. She turned away from it.

'So down below,' she said, 'that's what I want to see, I want to see the cabins.' The man pointed and led her down another small staircase, into the heart of the vessel.

'There are two cabins here at the rear, one for the master, one for the other guest. There's a couple of bunks at the side here. There's only five of us on board—there's plenty of room. And here's the galley.'

Clarissa made a point of stopping and standing, looking at each item before walking up and opening up the cupboard doors. 'You don't mind if I have a look about?'

'As long as you don't mind me having a look about,' said the man. Clarissa nearly wretched, but instead, she turned around and made a giggle, laughing at the man, as she opened up the cupboard doors in front of her. Inside were pots, pans, cups, nothing of interest, and she felt a hand on her backside.

'Is everything to your satisfaction?' said the man.

'I'm fine with it,' she said. 'Sometimes it's nice to be noticed,' and with that, she walked off towards the cabins. She opened the master's cabin and stepped inside to see a small bed and a desk.

'Best not spend too long in here,' said the man. 'Come on.'

'What's your name?' asked Clarissa, as once again his hand moved across her backside.

'George,' said the man, but Clarissa could tell clearly it wasn't, the insincerity in the voice and a sudden apprehension about being in the master's cabin giving him away. 'Probably best if you look in the other cabin,' said the man. 'You could spend longer in there. Captain of the boat won't be happy if he finds us in here.'

'Indeed,' said Clarissa. She walked into the second, slightly smaller cabin and found a bunk tight to the wall, a small desk, and a number of pictures up on the wall. Lying open was a project book, and smack in the middle of it was a photo of Aaron's Rod. There were other photos and images around the room. Then she noticed a picture of Howie Lemon. 'Somebody's busy in here,' said Clarissa. 'I just want over to look at the fixings on the back of that table.'

With that, she leaned over, looking across at the far end of the table. What this allowed her to do was to clock some notes below her. Again, they clearly referred to Aaron's Rod.

From behind her, she felt the man put his hands on her hips and pull himself close to her. If she hadn't been working cover, the guy would have felt a punch right to the jaw. Instead, she stood upright, turned around, planted a kiss right on the cheek of the man.

'So, we won't get into trouble if we're in this cabin; who's in this cabin then?'

'He's called Craig,' said George, almost forgetting himself. 'We were just told to bring him here. I don't know much about that.'

'Certainly likes his antiques,' said Clarissa, and with that, she wrapped herself around George planting a kiss on him and placing her hand on his backside.

She kissed him for about a minute, putting hands inside the pockets of his jeans acting as if she was a teenager. When she broke off, she gave his backside a gentle smack before she felt the hand.

'I'm sure there's beds available,' said the man. 'Or we could use one of mine. It's a bunk bed but I'm sure we wouldn't need a lot of room.'

Clarissa stepped back slightly. 'George, I'm a married woman. You let me see the inside of the boat, and for that you get a little kiss. Give me the boat and we might get to go to bed.' She gave a laugh and marched off out of the cabin, making her way back up to the outer deck of the boat, hurriedly followed by the man. She jumped off onto the quayside and turned around.

'Thank you. I'll tell my husband to get that. It looks exquisite.'

'Maybe next time I'll get the boat for you.'

'Indeed. The man you brought here, just so I don't say anything in front of the girls in case he's close by, what does he look like?'

'Why would you tell them about this?'

'I've just jumped on a boat and snogged a handsome sailor,' said Clarissa. 'At my age, that's a win.'

The man described the black-haired individual dressed in blue jeans with a crisp blue t-shirt. 'He's slightly smaller than me,' said the man.

Around five feet eleven thought Clarissa. 'Maybe next time I'll bring the girls back for a look,' she said to the man and left.

'Next time, come along and see how long we've got. I think you might need to see the cabins again.' Clarissa turned, walked away forcibly jiggling her backside as she went. When she got clear of sight of the vessel, she brushed back her hair almost as if she were cleaning the man out from it. *Wait till Macleod hears this*, she thought and picked up her phone looking for a signal.

Chapter 19

Clarissa switched off her phone, put it inside her pocket, and sat down on the harbour wall. Macleod had all the information, and he would be sending teams over immediately. All she had to do was wait. But something inside Clarissa didn't feel right. When she was running her own investigations, she wouldn't hang around like this. She should be off trying to find the man, making sure he didn't go any further out of town, and was worried in case he disappeared.

Macleod was probably just playing her with kid gloves, putting a soft barrier around her, but she didn't need it. After all, he sent her over here because although it might have been a bit of a wild goose chase, he had a feeling about this boat. There was nothing else to learn from the boat itself, so it wouldn't hurt if Clarissa started looking around at the town and tried to find the man who the crew had brought to Lochinver.

Clarissa jumped off the wall, walked along the seafront, and started disappearing into every small shop she could find. Lochinver was not that big. A fishing port on the west coast, it didn't take long for her to make her way across the few pubs and shops that were open at that time. The day was starting to lose its grip with the night beginning to move in when Clarissa walked into a pub at the far end of Lochinver. Even in summer, there was a fire on in the far corner, and she settled down, ordering a brandy.

Strictly, she shouldn't drink when on duty, but she couldn't very well sit there with a lemonade. It wouldn't look the part, and they were never that bothered on the arts team. If you could keep in character was all that mattered.

She took a seat close to the fire and scanned the inhabitants of the friendly pub. There was a family of four eating, and beyond them a group of three men, who looked like tradesmen having their evening meal after a day's work. Maybe they were lodging upstairs. They certainly looked nothing like the man she was wanting. It was as she was finishing her sweep across the uncrowded bar that she saw in the far corner, a pair of hands tucking into a piece of bread on the table.

Rather than move around to have a proper nosy at the person, Clarissa sat, bided her time, waiting for some excuse to check out the person that sat there. She saw a TV on the far wall and reckoned it was right about time for the news. She stood up and went over to the bar, requesting the channel be changed. From the corner of her eye, she caught a glimpse of the man eating the bread at the table.

Her heart skipped a beat. The trousers, the hair, the jacket. It was all good, all fitting the man's description that she'd received from the boat. Smiling, she thanked the woman behind the bar for changing the channel and made her way back to her seat, sitting down and slowly sipping her brandy. She watched the pair of hands, negotiating the food on the table for the next half an hour, waiting for them to make a move.

It seemed the man was going to be there for the night, for after finishing his meal, he approached the bar and ordered a couple of whiskeys before sitting down and slowly making his way through each one. Clarissa's own brandy seemed to last a lifetime. As she was just thinking she'd have to order another one, the man stood up, politely thanked the woman at the bar for her service, and left. Clarissa slowly counted. She didn't want to appear at the door behind the man, especially if he stopped to look around. She needed to be behind in a good fashion, able to tail in such a way that the man wouldn't think he was being followed.

It was early summer and the streetlights had not yet come on. It was not as bright as day, but there was certainly a decent twilight in the evening. Clarissa could easily watch the man make his way through town. She stayed back a good distance until she saw the man pick up a car at the far end of town. Before stepping into the red vehicle, he opened the boot, looked inside and then slammed it shut. Clarissa's own car was behind her, so she double-tailed back quickly, getting inside and driving quickly to the edge of town.

She hoped he wouldn't be that quick, but his car was out of sight, so she took the only route out of town. It was a number of corners before she sighted him, and she slowly followed the car. Clarissa knew they were heading south, and when the man turned into a car park just off the side of the road, she refrained from following him into it. Instead, taking the car a little further south, she parked it on a sidetrack that left the main road.

In a move that she was used to, Clarissa left her warrant card in the car, always worried that if she got frisked, having her ID on her would give her away instantly. Not that she was planning to engage with any suspects, but you just never knew which way things could go. With woods around her, she followed the road

163

back some five hundred metres to where the man had turned into the car park. She cut off into the forest just before the car park, so she could move in among the trees and observe the man without being seen. There was only one car, the red one she had seen the man drive, and he was sitting on the bonnet, almost impatient.

Clarissa decided she needed to get closer. If the man were here to meet someone, she wanted to get all the information she could from that meeting, especially if they knew where the item was. Having seen the man check his boot, Clarissa had a distinct feeling that Aaron's Rod might be on scene. Of course, he could have just been checking for a weapon. Maybe a rifle, or shotgun, kept out of sight. With that feeling rolling around her gut, she carefully made her way around the woods, determined to stay out of sight until she was only some thirty feet from the car, hidden behind a large oak.

The man had started to whistle, evidently quite at ease with what he was doing. Maybe he was a fence of some sort and this was run of the mill to him, somebody who moved things on. But with the price of the item and the significance of it, and also the number of people that died around it, he would do well to stay cool.

Clarissa heard the noise of a car engine and when she peered out from behind the oak, she saw a small dust cloud as the vehicle entered the car park. It wasn't a tarmac surface but rather comprised of loose stone and dusty mud. It was a cheap car park, made for the few numbers of people who would come out to these woods. A little rough and ready, it was an ideal meeting place. You could be virtually undisturbed. If you really wanted a private talk, you could disappear off into the woods themselves. Places like this were often used by courting couples as well. Clarissa was surprised that no one was here, especially for such a pleasant evening.

The new car was white, a long saloon, and pulled up opposite the red car. The man jumped off the bonnet, moved around to the side of his own car, and opened the driver's door almost keeping it in front of him like some sort of shield.

'Good evening,' said a woman, exiting the white car. Clarissa watched her stand up and saw someone in good shape. There was a confidence to the woman, and unlike the man, she emerged out into the open, not looking to hide behind any particular object. She had pulled from the car a large duffel bag and was now carrying it over her shoulder.

'One item for collection. Do you have the payment?'

The man nodded, disappeared round to the back of his red car, opening the boot. He emerged with a large bag of his own, a grey rucksack, and he took it to behind the open driver's side car door.

'That's not very friendly. I'm here to let you have the goods. It's just a friendly exchange. There's no need for that,' said the woman. 'I take it you've not done this sort of thing before.'

The man looked offended but once again, he didn't speak.

'Your client must be happy. Please, have a look and verify if you want.' The woman approached the red car, opened her own bag, placed her stuff on the car bonnet. It was an incredibly brazen move. From the distance she was looking from, Clarissa believed that it was Aaron's Rod. The man from the red car made his way slowly around to the front of his own car but only when the woman moved back towards hers.

Clarissa checked her watch. Macleod should be here soon. She could maybe phone but it was awkward at the moment. Maybe she should text. She made a quick press of buttons on her mobile, sending a message, hoping there would be a signal. Once that was done, she slipped her mobile back into her jeans pocket, and stood watching the scene unfold.

The woman seemed happy, letting the man check the item, and then when he turned around and picked up his own grey bag, she seemed to almost beam. The exchange was happening. If Macleod and the rest weren't here soon, Clarissa might have to act. She decided to get closer and scurried around a couple of trees trying to catch anything that might be said.

As she'd got into her new position, Clarissa was able to focus more clearly on the item on the bonnet and her eyes opened. This was it. This was the Rod, at least from medieval times. It was beautiful. Its jewels were dim with the little light that was still gleaming in the world. She stepped forward just a touch to try to get a better view and then cursed as her foot made a twig snap and the woman looked around quickly.

'Have you got someone with you? What is this? You were meant to be alone.'

'I'm alone,' said the man. 'There's nobody here. Probably just a bird or something.'

Clarissa tried to slink back inside, crouching behind a tree, but she heard the woman start to move, circling out wide. Then she saw Clarissa. Making eye to eye contact, the woman's hand went down to her hip, pulled out a gun and pointed it at Clarissa. 'Don't move. I'll shoot. You, at the bonnet. Step back. Why is she here? What's going on?'

'She's not with me,' said the man, but the woman had moved over closer to him, spun him around, and pushed his head down onto the bonnet of the car.

'Don't lie to me. You were just going to come and take it. I wasn't getting this money, was I? You can tell your boss he's not getting it.'

'The money. The money's in the bag,' said the man.

'The money's irrelevant. I can't trust you. You've double-crossed me. Who is she? Why is she here?'

'I told you, I don't know,' said the man. Clarissa stepped out from behind the tree, and the woman called her over closer. Raising her hands. Clarissa slowly stepped forward. The woman strode towards her and started to frisk her. Her purse was thrown on the ground, as was her mobile phone.

'She doesn't belong to you?' said the woman. 'I don't believe that for a minute. Is there anybody else around here? Anyone else?'

Clarissa could see she was becoming paranoid, spinning here and there, looking around her, but Clarissa also saw the man edge away from the bonnet and run to the inside of his own car. The woman, frantically looking around the car park, had taken her eye off the man. Clarissa saw him reach inside, and she knew what was coming.

'Don't. Don't do that.'

Then everything was a blur. Clarissa saw the man's hand come up above the car door, a handgun ready to fire. She saw the woman react quickly and with devastating force. Two shots fired quickly, both with a silencer on the end of the gun. The man's shoulder twisted, his legs lifted, and then hit the underside of the car door and he fell to the floor.

The woman ran quickly around the door, taking the man's gun and kicking it away. She then pointed her gun at Clarissa, who remained with her hands up in the air, desperate not to get shot herself.

'You, in the car,' said the woman. 'Take the bag on the bonnet with you.'

Clarissa did as she was told, picking up the Rod in a moment that should have been wondrous, but instead, she was fearing for her life, her body shaking. She got into the car, holding the rod between her legs and the woman joined her.

'Is he dead?' asked Clarissa.

'He should be, but I only hit him on the shoulder. He's not going anywhere. Besides, they need to get a message. I don't deal like this.'

'What on earth are you talking about?' asked Clarissa.

'Sit there and don't move,' said the woman. 'We're going for a little ride.' Clarissa watched the woman switch on the engine and she began to slowly drive the car from the car park.

'You don't want to do this,' said Clarissa. 'You don't. Just stop. Just—' The woman lashed out, catching Clarissa's face with her handgun. Everything went black.

Chapter 20

Macleod stood at the harbour side in Lochinver, the streetlights now on. With the bright darkness of summer now having taken over, it felt almost like a permanent dusk. Without electric light in the town, you could see well, but Macleod was worried. He had a call from his sergeant advising him that she had discovered the man who'd been on the boat in the harbour. Sally's Tan had brought him from Aberdeen, but on arrival, his sergeant was nowhere to be seen. Clarissa was uncontactable on her mobile phone. It simply rang out. When he rang her smaller one, the one that she'd kept in her shoe, there was no reply either.

The rest of the team had arrived as well. Ross marshalling members of the local force, but even they had driven in from a distance.

'I don't like it, Hope. Why is she not answering? I want you to get in the car and start fanning out. Get Ross to go north, you go south. Follow the road, see if you see anything suspicious. Her car isn't even here. We'll get the constables to start asking around in the bars, and the shops or wherever else is still open. We'll knock the doors and get people up if we have to. I take it we have a photo of Clarissa.'

'Pulled the one up from the station, sir. Not a problem.'

'Why's she gone off like this? I told her to sit tight, we'd be here. I had a hunch about this thing, Hope.'

'She's used to doing things on her own. That's the way she operated. She wasn't part of a team. That's what Ross said. Whenever he worked with her, she led.'

'Yes, but these guys could be dangerous. Extremely dangerous. Deadly. We've had murders already. I doubt they'll hesitate to pick off a police officer if she's in their way.'

'She's smarter than that, Seoras. Don't panic. I'll get in the car and go south. I'll speak to Ross. We'll get her. Don't worry.'

Macleod wished he shared Hope's feelings, but inside him was a dread. He should have been over here with her. He should have come along, but she was an experienced sergeant. She'd been in the force a while. There's just something when you worked in the murder squad though. You assumed everybody you interviewed, everybody around you, could at any point, kill. It sharpened you, you took fewer risks. Thieves and robbers were never quite the same, let alone those that messed about in the art world. Macleod stood wondering what he should do. Ross would coordinate.

'Hope,' he stuttered, 'bring the car here. I'm coming with you.'

'Seoras?'

'You heard me. I'm coming with you. I'm not sitting on my arse here.'

When Hope pulled up in the car, Macleod climbed in. He watched the constables going about their work as Hope drove out of Lochinver. They had managed to pull together ten officers, a significant number. But Macleod looked at the countryside around him. Lochinver was over on the west coast and there was so little about, so many areas you could go and hide in woods, open land. Even around the coastal area, you could come down to small beaches, crags, nooks. If something had happened, who knew where she was? Macleod felt his arms begin to tense; his fists gripped together.

'Easy, Seoras. You're putting me an edge, and I'm trying to drive.'

'Just keep your eyes peeled.'

Hope continued along the winding road and drove into a car park beside Culag woods. There was a single car with its door laying open. It was red and seemingly abandoned.

'Pull up, Hope. That doesn't look right.' As she stopped the car, Macleod jumped out and his eyes began to pick up in the darkness a figure on the floor. He ran over and he realized there was a man lying prone. He reached down quickly to the man's neck with his fingers. The skin was cold and there was no pulse.

'Ambulance here now, Hope. Get on the blower.' Macleod fell down again. No, there was nothing, but he knew the routine. He put his hands on the man's chest and began doing CPR. After five minutes, there was nothing, and Hope was standing over him.

'He's gone, Seoras,' said Hope. 'Did you recognize him at all?'

'No,' said Macleod, 'but he's been shot. Twice, by the looks of it. Didn't finish him off though. Looks like he's bled out.'

'There's been tire tracks here. Another car.'

'Okay. We'll phone Jona; see what she can discover.' Macleod stood up, made his way across to the car and began to look inside, careful not to touch anything. As he moved to the other side, he realized there was a bag on the floor. Putting on some gloves, he opened it carefully and saw a large quantity of money there.

'Hope, over here. Look.' McGrath joined him. She blew a large whistle when she saw the amount of cash sitting in the bag.

'We better look after that until somebody gets here. I'll call Ross. There's no sign of Clarissa though.'

'There's been an exchange here. There's the money, but there's no item. One car. I don't know who this guy is. Whether he has brought the item and they've taken it and then dumped the money with him, but something's clearly gone wrong. We need to find Clarissa; this is getting out of hand.'

'Try her mobile again, sir. See if that brings up anything.' Macleod tried Clarissa's number again on both mobiles. He rang her small one first, in her shoe. It rang out, but when he rang the second one, he could hear a ringtone around the car park. Hope picked up a phone. 'It's here, Seoras. It's here. She's been here, and yet her car is not.'

'Someone's got her, Hope. Someone must have her.'

* * *

It was two hours later, and Macleod was sitting in a tent in the car park, a makeshift base. All the services had been called, and a search was beginning of the surrounding area, but Macleod was not hopeful. He doubted this search was going to find anything. Anybody holed up with Clarissa would soon see them coming, and probably high-tail it out of there before anyone arrived or worse still, they might dispose of her as unnecessary baggage.

One thing that occurred to Macleod was, "Why was Clarissa still alive?" Maybe it was because she was a policewoman. Then again, they found her car safe beyond the car park, her warrant card still in it. Maybe it's because they didn't think she was a policewoman. If the buy had gone wrong, maybe they wanted a hostage, someone to stop retaliation.

He swept this hand through his hair and could feel the sweat on it. It was cold. He realized that his nerves were starting to get the better of him. Macleod hated this. It was like a needle in the haystack. Nowhere to go.

He had asked for a phone check to be done, given the seriousness of his colleague's situation, but the phone company said that while it had been registered just south of Lochinver, it had dropped out from the mast. The small phone was no longer in contact. On the bright side, the phone hadn't stopped completely, hadn't been destroyed, and Macleod was hoping the signal loss was because Clarissa had simply moved out of mobile range. He had to also be aware that maybe someone had discovered the phone hidden away in her shoe heel.

'Coffee for you, Seoras. Any more ideas?' Hope was wearing a large frown. She was as frustrated as he was. Hope had spent the last hour and a half on the boat, Sally's Tan, interviewing the crew, but she quickly found out that they were not anyone special. Sure, they got hired to move things around and ask no questions. Whenever Hope mentioned Lord Argyle, they shook their heads. Maybe they were too far down the chain. They gave a description of the man they'd carried, and it perfectly matched the body that was lying in the car park. They had no idea what he was going to do, but Hope had gone on board and started to search through the cabins.

One of the men said he had shown a woman through earlier. When Hope had pressed him for a description of the woman, he mentioned the purple hair, and she knew that Clarissa had

173

been on board. That was where they'd last spoken with her. She'd come off, told Macleod everything, and he had told her to wait.

Macleod looked up and saw Ross coming over in a hurry.

'Spoke to the lady at the bar, sir. She remembers Clarissa being in there. A purple-haired woman following a man over the bar after watching him for a couple of hours. She's given me a description, and that's the body in the car park. Looks to me like she was off for a meet, tailed him down. Whatever's happening, something has gone wrong. I just hope to God, she's not involved in it. Maybe she's heading off, tailing the woman.'

'She's probably a hostage, Ross. We have to get used to that fact,' said Macleod. 'We're searching everywhere; we're putting the feelers out. There's nothing else we can do, except wait until we find something.'

'When you spoke about Lord Argyle, have you got anybody watching him and his people?'

'Got straight on to Dundee and Aberdeen, put the wheels in motion. Told them we don't know where our girl is though. At this point, but he's not likely to sully himself.'

Macleod took himself away from the tent getting himself away from all activity. He stood looking up at night sky and felt a tap on his shoulder. Turning around, he saw Hope.

'Are you okay? It's not like you just to drift off.'

'I'm fine, Hope. We'll not find her this way, though. Why'd she have to go and do this? Stewart wouldn't have done this.'

'Stop,' said Hope. 'Can't do that. She's not Stewart. Stewart would never have gotten to this position. She basically flirted with a guy on the boat to find out all the details. Clarissa is an operator, wait and see. She's smart and she's savvy. Trust me, sir.'

Macleod nodded, but it was only half-hearted. 'It's pretty peaceful out here, isn't it,' said Macleod, suddenly. 'Did you ever wish you'd gone to these places when it wasn't work?'

'What do you mean, sir?' asked Hope.

'Like here. Just sit with the stars with that man of yours. You wouldn't rather just lay back here and sit all night looking up at the stars?'

'I can think of other things I'd do all night with him,' said Hope cheekily. Macleod turned and gave a stare. 'Sorry. Too coarse for the moment we're in, was it?'

'We need to get her, Hope. We need to get her. She was under my cover. I said I was going to look after her. I should have let you look after her; you'd have been with her.'

'For something as minor as this? A boat to check out? I would have sent her on her own,' said Hope. 'I wouldn't have done anything different.'

'Yes, you would. You'd have had the time to go. But no, I was going to inspect her, see she picked up all the important things but I didn't cover off the one fundamental thing that I should've done. Keep an eye on the new person until I learn all her traits. Learn about what she does.'

'She's probably just trying to solve it, sir. You wouldn't have stopped, you'd have kept going, especially if you had found him. That's probably what she did. Found them waiting for us, by the time we got organized to get people over here.'

'Don't try and make it into some sort of logistical nightmare. I didn't do it, I didn't cover her off, I didn't back her up. I should've been over here with her. She asked if she should take somebody with her. I said no. I didn't think it was going to be—'

'No, I don't think any of us thought it was going to be like that.'

'Try the phone company again,' said Macleod. 'See if they came up with anything else, and let's make sure we check the ambulance. Maybe that guy wasn't the only one that got shot.'

'Jona says there's only been two bullets found. His weapon wasn't fired.' Macleod nodded, but it was cold comfort. They needed to get Clarissa, and fast.

Chapter 21

Clarissa opened her eyes and felt the damp on her backside and thighs. Her back was up against a stone wall with her legs in front and on the floor was a puddle. At first, she worried that she had been so weak or unconscious, that she had passed fluid, but then she realized there was no smell of urine but instead, a dampness, almost mildew smell invaded her nostrils.

Her eyes revealed no mysteries, the room was simply dark and she struggled to hear anything. There was only a constant drip coming from the far side of the room as she calculated. Feeling an itch on her nose, she went to scratch it but found her hands cable-tied together. She could feel the thin plastic on her wrist and then trying to steady herself she looked to move her feet apart but could only adjust by spreading her knees giving herself that little bit of balance. Her feet were tied too.

Well, old girl, thought Clarissa, *you're really in the smelly stuff this time. You should have stopped at the art department.*' She thought she felt a breeze, a slight wind across her face. Maybe there was a door over there and she decided to try and shuffle towards it. With her feet out in front and her hands tied, she moved her bottom forward to try and do some sort of caterpillar motion. She tumbled to her right, cracked her head off a wall, and ended up just lying on the floor. She realized how long the puddle was now as her hair became drenched in the fluid. With her elbows and her knees, she worked herself back up to a sitting position and resigned herself not to move.

'Hello,' she shouted. 'Anyone?' There was nothing. Clarissa bowed her head taking in deep breaths to try and stop any agitation from growing. She had seen the woman shoot the man. *Was he dead? Possibly.* She was alive, but why? *What was it those Asian people did? Meditate, breathe, take it easy. Think through your thoughts, be at one.* All this wasn't Clarissa at all. She was all style, with a good deal of substance to be fair. She did everything with an air. She didn't sit still; she didn't relax. She went and she did it.

She thought of Macleod, of how he was going to be pissed at her. After all, she had gone off looking for a suspect; it wasn't her fault that everything moved, that he was slow getting people to the ground. Maybe she couldn't tell him that, maybe that wasn't the best career move if indeed there was a career left after this. She had to get out first, had to play it cool.

Clarissa thought about what was going on. *The man had turned up with money evidently to buy the rod; the woman then shoots him and takes it back thinking she's been double-crossed. How do I help her?* thought Clarissa *I'm tied up here. Hopefully, she doesn't know who I am, so how do I help her. She needs a buyer and maybe I can pose as a representative, a rival representative. I wasn't there as backup for the man. I was there to stop it, to get the rod before him. I'm able to offer money, get her to take me back towards my car.*

She pulled her legs up towards her, huddling herself in tight because she'd heard a noise. There was a rustling along the edge of the room. She'd heard it before staying in some dungeon-like housing in London. Mice climbed up the behind the walls and scurried under the floorboards. You could hear them in the ceiling too. Scritch-scratch, tiny feet tapping along. Clarissa hated mice with a passion.

Sitting in the dark, she felt the scratching was coming closer. And then something ran across her feet. It was light but ticklish. As she kicked her feet out hard, something ran across her lap. And then there was something up her back and then in her hair. She shook her head wildly, eventually managing to get the mouse off. But Clarissa could feel the cold sweat coming on.

Everyone has some phobia, some fear. She just had to be traditional and make it mice. She needed one of those cleaning ladies, the ones with the big broom, to just come in and whack them, like in the cartoons. You would see the mice flying across the room, smacking up against the wall before falling to the floor. Of course, they'd probably come back out with some ludicrous stick of dynamite, but you'd give anything for one of those women with the magic brush.

Clarissa blinked as the door opened and a bright light hit her face. There was a brief scurrying but in the opposite direction. And then Clarissa saw a figure enter through the door, crouching before her.

'Awake, are you? Good. Need to get some answers? Who are you?' Clarissa looked up and struggled to see who it was with the brightness coming through the door behind the woman, causing her to be silhouetted.

'I'm just a friend,' said Clarissa. A slap came across her face and she tumbled over to the side, cracking her head off the wall again. This time it stung and she thought she felt blood coming from beside her ear.

'Don't mess me about. I don't take kindly to that nonsense. Now, who are you?

Clarissa sniffed. She hauled herself back up into position. 'I said, I'm a friend.'

'There are no friends in this business.' Another slap to the cheek, but it wasn't so strong, and Clarissa was able to hold her position.

'I'm someone who can help you.'

'What we're you doing with the Blue Bird?'

'Blue Bird?' said Clarissa. 'I just jumped out?' And she cursed herself for it. She could have used the name acted like she knew who it was. After all, it wouldn't be difficult to work with it.

'Why were you in the car park? What were you doing there? Blue Bird brought me the money. But why were you there? Were you going to take it back there, to kill off me once you had the staff?'

'I wasn't there to take it off you. I was there to give you a counteroffer. But unfortunately, things got a little out of hand.'

'Wasn't anything I couldn't handle.' said the woman almost nonchalantly.

'You didn't seem to handle it that well. He's dead and you've left the money. Why didn't you take it with you?' asked Clarissa.

'You don't operate in this game, love, do you? You take the money after killing him and they may come after you. He's probably nothing to them. But they will want their money back, especially if they haven't got the item.'

Clarissa nodded. 'I'm here to offer you a sum of money for the item.'

'You've a funny way of showing it, hiding out, and you've cost me a buyer. That would've gone through.'

'Don't be so sure. There are probably more people there. Once you kill them, they scarper. Nothing like the arrival of the boys in blue to chase anyone away.'

'I think you're winding me up. Should just kill you here and now.'

'Kill me and they'll find me, and they'll come for you.'

'They'll never find you here, not this far down. Strange place this, been able to hide out for a while now. Of course, I've got the most salubrious room next door. I didn't think I'd need this one, what with the water in it and that. The mice, too. Next door's a bit cosier, but I think I'll leave you here. If you're not unpleasant to me I might even simply shoot you rather than leave you to rot.'

Clarissa's heart thumped. The woman was looking to do it, wasn't she? Looking to end her.

'You don't want to do that; my buyer would pay you double what you had coming.'

'Is your buyer worth millions then?' asked the woman.

'My buyer is Lord Argyle. You know he's quite a big acquirer of antiques, maybe some of your fellow workers in the industry would be able to point him out to you. He asked me to come and inquire into purchasing the Rod. You don't want to leave him disappointed.'

'So, where's your money then?' asked the woman.

'Back in the car. You're lucky you ran into me. You need to make contact though. Need to let me set it up through my broker. Do that and you might even have it by the end of tonight. You can walk away in the morning with whatever price you name.'

'I think I could get a couple of million for this in an auction, at least. But I'm not greedy, we'll call it two million. How do you contact him?'

'I am what you might call a finder's fee. I don't talk to the man direct. I need you to put me in contact with a dealer—he works out of Pitlochry.'

'And what, this dealer will contact and set up?'

'I'll give you a number to ring. One to talk on so you can make proper arrangements. You can send it all over in text message and he'll be here. He's desperate for it, bit of a fanatic.'

'You better not be lying to me. I'll do to you what I did to the man in the car park. I took Bluebird down because of you.'

'It wasn't my fault he went for a gun,' retorted Clarissa and then suddenly backed off with her attitude. The woman's voice was becoming more and more serious.

'I think you're a liar.' said the woman and backed out of the small room closing the door behind her, leaving Clarissa in the dark.

'Lord Argyle,' she shouted. 'That's who you want and I can get him.' The holding pen went silent again. Clarissa listened out carefully for mice. Hopefully, they had all fled.

Clarissa lay in the dark for at least an hour and then heard someone coming back. The door opened and she was hit by the bright light again, unable to see who was in front of her. 'Well, looks like I'm running out of options,' said the woman who had just entered. 'I need to get a hold of Lord Argyle because this piece is getting too hot. You've got police everywhere. How are they going to get here?'

'Let me deal with that. You just need to get me out somewhere with a phone signal.'

'Okay,' said the woman, 'Why don't you come now?'

'It's a bit hard with the feet and the hands tied up.'

Clarissa saw a knife being brandished, its outline against

the light behind her. She hacked off four of the plastic tags. Clarissa was able to move forward on her knees out of the room. She found herself in a stone corridor and opposite there was a room with an open door and a similar stone dungeon to her own except that there was no water here. She pushed along off several stone steps and came out at the top of a small room. 'The signal is good here,' said the woman.

'Well, if you let me get my mobile, I'll just give them a—'

'No,' said the woman, 'You don't do that here.'

She reached into her back pocket and pulled out a mobile phone. 'This one's clean, never been used. One call, I hope you know his number.'

Clarissa knew his number all right. Arthur Dicken was a dealer that Clarissa had dealt with maybe fifteen to twenty years ago. He had retired but she had his home number. The man must nearly be hitting retirement, but he was still in the know and more than that, he could spill the right line to lure the girl. Clarissa prayed he would still be living at the same address or at least carry the same number. With her hands still tied together, she punched in the numbers on the mobile and then lifted the earpiece up to her ear.

The phone kept ringing and at first, Clarissa became extremely worried. Her life was probably hanging on the fact that someone needed to answer the phone. A few moments later the call was picked up. Clarissa breathed a sigh of relief. Then a voice she recognized from long ago came on. 'This is Dicken Arthur; how can I help you?'

'Arthur,' said Clarissa, 'It's me, Annie.'

Annie had been the name Clarissa had been going by back in the day when she first dealt with Arthur Dicken. The guy was a rogue and he had gone down for a little bit of time, but Clarissa had never broken cover as she let the others have the arrest and the man trusted her implicitly.

'What can I do for you, Annie? It's been a long time.'

'I've got your retirement pension sorted. Do you know the stuff that's going around at the moment?'

'No, you haven't. No way,' said Arthur.

'I need to get it to a buyer. I heard Lord Argyle is after it. Tell him I've got it. Tell him you trust me. But he needs to move as we've got heat. Cops are all over us at the moment.'

Clarissa hung up the phone and handed it back to the woman. 'You never told me your name.'

The woman looked at her and nodded. 'You're right. I didn't. If you want, you can call me Missy.'

'Missy,' said Clarissa, ''what you have to realize is that this guy's a good option for you. He's a big player. With the money he'll pay you can go anywhere in the world. They won't come for you.'

'Well, I hope not. Because when we go to meet him, you'll be coming with me with a gun in your back. Until then, it's back inside you go.' Clarissa was led back down this long passage through the roof, forcibly thrown in.

'If he doesn't come back in the next couple of hours, I might have to leave here,' Missy announced. ''And you, the only way you'll be leaving here is in a body bag.''

Chapter 22

Macleod watched as one of the search teams was returning back to the base station in the car park south of Lochinver. Hope was standing close to a search coordinator. Macleod had seen her face, first rising in a brief moment of wonder, and then falling as a result of "nothing found" was passed. Hope had stayed close to those coordinating the search, giving brief updates to Macleod as it went.

Seoras prefer to remain aloof, trying to think through possibilities and actions rather than get bogged down in where to look. He wasn't the specialist in that front—better for others to do that. Now he watched Hope trudge over towards him, face dejected, her red hair still tied up in the ponytail, but even that seemed limp, hanging at the side of her neck.

'No change then, nothing found?' asked Macleod.

'No, Seoras. They could be well out of here by now. Jump in a car and just go; who knows where they could have taken her, but we keep looking, we need to.'

'Stay with it, Hope. I want to know the moment anything is found there. Keep getting an idea of what they've discovered. They might not necessarily recognize something as being important, and I want our people on top of it.'

'Of course. Of course, I will Seoras. It's just well—.' Hope trudged back off to the search teams. For being summer, the early hours of the morning were still chilly. Macleod had put a large jacket on him. An occasional cup of coffee had been brought to him and as he sat looking out onto the night sky that was quickly turning to morning, he tried to envisage how this would play out.

He hated the waiting, just hated it. He had a brief update from those he had assigned to look after the various family members of the team. All was well, no one had been targeted, all was quiet. At least that was something. He tried at times to console himself with the knowledge that Clarissa knew what she was getting into, well as much as any of them ever did. Inside, he kept beating himself up; he should have been more forceful with instructions. He probably should have sent Hope over instead. As he was half wandering around the car park, Ross came racing up to him.

'Boss, boss, just got a phone call in from the mobile phone company. There's been a partial signal, we've tracked it, it's north of here.'

'How specific can we be with it?'

'Well, it was on the mast for quite a while, so it's about a hundred-metre square.'

'Out here, Ross, a hundred-metre square has probably got nothing in it. That's terrific, come on. Where is it?'

'I'm just getting the coordinates now. Tell Hope to grab the car.'

It was really Macleod's instruction to give, but he didn't mind as he watched Ross run off to firm up exactly where they needed to look. Of course, there was a search team coming with him, and the minibuses prepared to race up the road in their wake. About two minutes later, a car pulled up. The passenger door was flung open and as Macleod stepped into it, he saw a changed woman inside. Hope was buzzing again, finally having somewhere to go, some lead to follow, instead of waiting around.

'Ross is coming too,' said Macleod. 'Over there by the exit of the car park. Grab him. Let's go.'

'Should we wait for the entourage, for the search party?'

'No, if we all turn up at once, they're going to get spooked if they're still there. We get there first, you never know; we might catch them before they leave.'

'Yes, boss.' Hope put her foot down on the accelerator, the car wheel spinning slightly on the gravelly surface before it was propelled out onto the main road. Macleod watched as they passed through the town lights of Lochinver and began heading north, back out into the countryside. A kilometre north of Lochinver, the road split left and right and Ross leaned forward from the backseat, shouting at Hope to turn left.

'It's about another two kilometres along, near a place called Rhicarn.'

Hope spun the wheel. Driving along what was essentially a non-marked single-track road, her headlights were on, but in truth, anybody in the way was just going to have to shift. Macleod's hand was involuntarily held out in front of him, and he dared not look at the dial which he believed would be reading at least eighty. For all that, Hope was not reckless. She took the corners as someone trained in advanced driving would, slowing down into them and accelerating back out. Small trees passed on either side and it was difficult to tell where the road would go next. Hope kept her foot down, ensuring that they would arrive at the scene well before the minibus of searchers could manage.

They drove along the road and Ross pointed left at the small turnoff in towards a house. They passed through a number of trees and into a large bed and breakfast, but Ross pointed to her the road that went on past the building.

'In there,' he shouted. Hope kept driving until a gate stopped her advance.

'Everyone out,' said Macleod. The three of them hopped over the fence taking the steel gate in their own particular mannerism.

Macleod, one foot on, swung a leg over, found the other side and then dropped down. Hope simply placed two hands on one side and strung her legs over the top and back down. Ross ran up, leaned over, put his arm down and swung his legs over the top of his head and back down onto the ground. His two deputies were well ahead of him by the time Macleod was running in the same direction.

'Here somewhere,' said Ross. 'It's here.' They stopped at a large field with a number of trees around the edge, but there seemed to be nothing. The sun was beginning to rise to a more substantial level now. While it was not full daylight, most things could be seen well and Macleod saw a stone cover setting proud from the ground.

'What's that, Ross?'

'I don't know, sir. I'll check it.' The three of them ran hard across to it. When Macleod arrived, Ross was looking down at a stone square trying to move it forcefully with his hands. 'It's not moving, sir.'

'Never mind that,' said Macleod. 'What's that?' Another eighty metres on was a very small stone turret coming out of the ground.

'Promising, that's what that is,' said Hope. She took off before the men could catch up with her. Macleod saw her enter what was effectively a small stone circular tower and as he arrived, he saw steps descending into the ground. The steps also ran up above him but given that he saw no one on top of the building, he thought the best bet was to look down.

'Sir, down here.' Macleod clambered down steps that were too awkward to run down, the size almost just too big for a human to walk comfortably with. As he reached the front of the stairs, he saw a stone passage in front of him. It was dark and he took out a penlight but he saw Hope had already entered.

'People have been in here, sir,' said Hope.

As Macleod joined her in what was a small dormitory, he saw a flask, smelt coffee, and clocked the brand of the food packets on the ground. He spun out from that room and looked at the room across, where a door was lying half-open. Stepping inside, he smelled mildew. The place had obviously had water issues in this part of the building and was soaked through. He heard his feet splash as his pen flashed around, and mice were running for a corner. Hope appeared on his shoulder.

'All empty, Seoras. This could be anything but there was food so it may be something. However, it looks like they've gone.'

'But gone where?' asked Macleod. 'Why would you use a phone? You're hiding out here? What's the point?'

'How do you mean, Seoras?'

'Boss,' interrupted Ross, 'if you read the document stating about the phone call it, said that the signal from Clarissa's shoe, the mobile phone in it, came from roughly this direction but these precise coordinates come from a phone that was in service at roughly the same time. Given that there's not that many phones around here, the phone company put two and two together and gave us both call details but the other call is longer, that's why it's so accurate to this position.'

'It could be somebody else then.'

'It could,' said Macleod, 'but look at this place. Look at this,' he said bending down he moved this pen torch and shone his light on a little piece of plastic lying on the ground. 'That's a cable tie. It's been cut. Somebody didn't do a good job of tidying up.'

'But they're gone,' said Hope, 'and where?'

'But they haven't gone far,' said Macleod. 'The least we can do is get up, start getting the cars about, see if we can find anyone on the move.' Staring down at the piece of plastic in his hand, Macleod thought hard about what was happening while Hope disappeared to head upstairs and talk to the search team.

'What is it, sir?' asked Ross.

'They made a phone call here. That says to me that there was something to talk about. Maybe a switch. It could be getting rid of Clarissa or they could be making a play for the Rod. Whoever's got the Rod, of course, but I think it's sitting here with whoever is keeping Clarissa captive and they want to get rid of it. Too many bodies dying and they haven't gotten their money.' As Macleod stood there, pen torch focused on the piece of plastic, he could hear a distant sound, sounding like a rush of wind. Drums beating in the distance coming closer but more mechanical.

'Do you hear that Ross, or is it just me?'

'No, sir. Your hearing is fine. I hear that too.'

'What's the time?' asked Macleod.

'I make it, oh, four in the morning.'

'That's a helicopter, isn't it?'

'Yes, sir, it is.'

Macleod dropped the piece of plastic, turned quickly, and started walking up the steps back out of the stone structure. 'Ross, who flies at 4:00 a.m. this low in these parts?'

'I'm not sure sir.'

'Neither am I.' Macleod continued up to the top of the tower, only one-story high. He took out his mobile phone dialling a number he rarely had cause to ring. The senior air traffic controller answered it.

'This is Scottish Centre. Speaking to watch manager, Allen Forsythe. Who's speaking, please?'

'This is DI Macleod, based in Inverness. I'm on the west side at the moment. West coast just above Lochinver. Had a helicopter just go over the top of me. Do you have anything working in this area?'

'Just stand by, sir.' The phone went quiet. Macleod stood, his foot tapping, aware that an idea was forming in his head and the answer to whether or not he was correct would probably come in the next thirty seconds.

'Hello, Inspector, there's no aircraft working us in that area. The guys on the sector have said they did see a 7000 squawk go over, but it dropped off well before it got to the coastline.'

'How far before?' asked Macleod.

'Ten miles at least,' said the watch manager.

'Many thanks, sir.' Macleod put the phone down.

'What's that about?' asked Ross.

'That aircraft isn't talking to anybody. It had a squawk on, transponding so ATC will be able to see it. That got switched off ten miles ago.'

'But don't air traffic then try and get hold of it?'

'No,' said Macleod. 'That's just a squawk he put up to say,

here I am. You're perfectly entitled to switch it off, especially if you're small, but more importantly, you would switch it off if you were trying to hide what you were doing and where you were landing.'

Ross looked over and felt he was still just about able to see a red light flashing on the helicopter. 'It's up that way, sir.' Said Ross.

'Indeed, it is. Hope,' shouted Macleod, 'to the car, now.' Macleod took off as quick as he could back down the steps and started running for the car. As he reached the gate, Ross was already ahead of him. Hope, too. He heard the car engine running as he made a slow effort over the gate. The house they had passed by on the short driveway was now lit up and there was quite a commotion between some of the searchers and the residents of the building. Hope spun the car around, drove carefully past the many other cars that had arrived, and took off, back out onto the road.

'Left,' shouted Ross. 'Keep going left.'

'You still got eyes on, Ross?'

'Roughly, sir. Roughly, but it looks like it's heading up towards Storr.'

'Keep the foot going, Hope. Quick as you can, or we may be too late.'

'Too late for what?'

'It's either the switch, Hope, they're going to get the Rod and somebody is getting paid, or it's goodbye, Clarissa.'

Hope kept her foot down as the road bent this way and that, small and single track. Fortunately, at 4:00 a.m., there weren't many people around to prevent her driving quickly. She spun past the white houses with grey slated roofs, and Macleod found himself hanging on for grim life as they raced past. Soon they had arrived at Storr, but there was no sign of the helicopter.

'Keep going North, they certainly haven't come back,' shouted Macleod. As the road continued to twist and turn, Hope suddenly came across more junctions.

'Where do I go?' she cried.

'Ross?' asked Macleod.'

'Last place I saw it was to my left so go west, take left.'

'Keep going left,' said Macleod. 'If it's over that way, it's over towards the coast, it's probably near a beach, flat piece of ground, who knows,' The road then turned back and forward on itself, and once again, they passed sporadic houses. In the distance, Macleod caught one single light flashing, and a silhouette of a shape rounded at the top.

'Over there, Hope, keep going along the road over to there.'

'That's it, sir, anti-collision light, there's not going to be anybody else out here.'

Macleod looked down at the map he had on his lap, identifying where there was some flat land.

'Quick, or we may be too late.'

Chapter 23

Macleod traipsed his way over what was rough terrain towards a small river. His ploy was to come down the riverbed so he could get close to the participants and whatever exchange, or handover was going on. The ground was not totally flat, but from the contours on the map he'd been reading, he believed that the far side of the river might have a flat enough area for a helicopter to land and was also clear of any telegraph wires.

Together with Hope and Ross, he made his way, occasionally finding his foot falling in a small rabbit hole, but they kept delay to a minimum as they made their way across the field towards the riverbank, shielded from the meeting by a rise in the ground which formed a small hillock.

'Seoras,' whispered Hope, 'how do we do this? Are we just going to talk them down? The woman's probably got a gun. After all, she killed the guy in the car park. Or probably anyway.'

'I don't see any other way. We're not going to have time to get a squad here with weapons, but we'll play this tight. I'll be the main confronter. You and Ross are going to have to go in a pincer movement. Try and keep them contained, and above all, Hope, disable their helicopter. If they can't get airborne again, they won't do anything. They'll be stuck here, and we'll have plenty of people coming behind us to sort things out.'

'Just be careful,' said Hope. 'You give them no options, that gun could be used.'

'I've done this before. I do have a little bit of experience, Hope.'

'All the same, I don't want to see you dead, boss.'

Macleod pointed to Ross, sending him out wide while he took the stream and walked right down towards the patch of land where the helicopter had landed. Beyond him, he could hear voices and one of them sounded angry.

* * *

Clarissa stood, almost shivering, and she wasn't sure if the fear was making her shiver or if it was simply the cold. She watched the helicopter land, and now stepping out to it, she saw the face of a man she had pursued for so long. She'd never been able to pin anything on him and now here he was about to take a most expensive item from her and she was unable to do anything about it.

'Is that him?' asked the woman standing by Clarissa with a gun pointing into her back.

'That's Lord Argyle. It looks like he's brought some money with him, too,' said Clarissa. There were two men stepping out from the helicopter, one remaining in it, dressed in tartan trousers and a rather spectacular overcoat. The man at the front had white hair, a rather ostentatious moustache, and seemed to be beaming from ear to ear. Beside him, a tall dark fellow of some six-foot carrying two bags, one in each hand, large sports duffels.

'I take it you have the item,' said Lord Argyle.

'I take it there's cash in there.'

'I said I'll make the deal, and I'm here, and I expect to see what belongs to God.'

'God will have to pay us money,' said the woman. 'Put the two duffle bags over here, and I'll check them.'

'Is there any need for the gun?' asked Lord Argyle. 'You can see I'm unarmed. If you must, you can search me and my colleague.'

'No, you can just stay at a distance,' said the woman. 'Tell your man to drop the bags there and move over to the side. Once I've checked the money, you'll get your item.'

Clarissa was standing perfectly still, and that was because, behind her, the staff was resting against her back. The woman had brought it and placed it when the helicopter had landed, telling Clarissa not to move. Slowly, the woman made her way over, her gun pointed the whole time at Argyle. She unzipped the duffle bags, taking out bills of money, and checking them carefully. She then zipped the bags back up and brought them over towards Clarissa.

'I believe you may know this one,' the woman said, pointing at Clarissa.

'Indeed I do, and she's in a number of guises, I believe. Who are we today, Ms Urquhart?' Clarissa almost spat on the ground. The woman came along behind her, brought out the Rod, placing it in Clarissa's hands, and told her to walk forward to hand it over to Argyle. Clarissa's body was shaking, wondering if she'd be shot dead at the end of this. Another part of her was enraged. Why was such an item as this going to such a scoundrel? She needed to do something about it, but what could she do? It wasn't like the Rod had any power, did it?

Was there something she could ask for? Cry out? She wasn't religious anyway. It's not as if God would answer.

'That's it. Give it here,' said Argyle, snatching it out of Clarissa's reach.

There it was, her moment was taken. All her life, she had so little regard for religion, only the study of it in the historical sense. Just now, it felt like she was reaching out, praying for someone to come and help her out of the situation she was in.

'Now, if you don't mind,' a voice said out of sight. 'I think I'll be having that.' Clarissa turned, and from the small river, a man was appearing. He had on a long coat and was quite aged, but his eyes were penetrating, looking straight at Argyle.

'And who is this?' said Argyle.

'Detective Inspector Macleod, sir, and you are under arrest.'

'How dare you speak to someone holding the Rod of Aaron like that? You would dare to rebuke me when I hold such power in my hands?'

'If that is indeed a weapon of God, then it certainly won't work for you,' said Macleod. Clarissa watched as Argyle stepped forward, taking the Rod up in his hand, and crying out.

'Send this man out. Cast this villain from my face.' With that, he threw the Rod on the ground. There was a small clatter, and Macleod almost winced as one of the stones on top of the rod smashed.

'I don't think you wanted to do that.'

'Why?' shouted Argyle. 'Why? It should work. Rain down on him. Take this fiend from my face.'

The woman beside Clarissa was growing restless, and she pulled out her gun again. 'I don't need no power from God,' she said and stuck her gun to Clarissa's head. 'Inspector, pick up the staff, and give it to me.' Macleod, watching the gun carefully, bent down, and took the staff over to the woman holding Clarissa hostage. 'I'm going to make my way over to that helicopter,' she said. 'When I get inside, he's going to fly me somewhere. And, if nobody intervenes, you might get your officer back. If anyone tries to do anything funny, then she dies.' Macleod nodded and walked over with the staff, handing it to Clarissa.

Lord Argyle jumped up and down, raging, and began swearing at the woman, telling her it was God's to own, and not hers to take. She walked up to him, put her gun to his head. Then, at the last second, took it away, instead striking him with the butt across the head. He fell to the ground as his man ran towards him, but then stopped suddenly as the gun was put in his face.

'No, no, no,' said the woman. 'We go over towards the helicopter.'

Clarissa saw Macleod nodding gently, letting her know it was okay to go and not to struggle. The gun was placed, again, at the back of her head. She shook as she walked the steps towards the helicopter. Carefully, Clarissa climbed up into the rear of the four-seat helicopter. The woman followed her in, gun pointing in her hand, but looking back out the window.

'Fire up the engine, son. We're leaving.'

The pilot said nothing. Barely moving at all. 'I said, fire up the engine, son. Get us moving, or people around here are going to die. You may be the first one.'

That would be so stupid, thought Clarissa. *Why would you shoot the only person who can fly you out of here?* She knew it was an empty threat. Instead, Clarissa was more likely to die, more likely to be used as an example. The woman spun round suddenly in the seat, pointing the gun out of the helicopter.

'Back,' she shouted. Argyle had run up, trying to get close, blood streaming from his temple. Instead, Macleod walked past him, and stood several feet away from the helicopter, hands in the air.

'Just go,' he said. 'Take her and go. When you set down, let her go. There's no point implicating yourself in something. Have a bit of compassion. She has children and a husband.'

This, of course, was news to Clarissa, but she nodded appropriately, producing a tear in her eye.

'You come to this side,' the woman said, pulling Clarissa over, making her sit in the seat that was nearest to where Macleod was standing. 'You make a move, Inspector, I'll shoot her, and she'll drop from this helicopter at your feet. You understand me?' Macleod nodded.

Clarissa looked at him and saw a man full of confidence, but she didn't feel confident. Instead, the cold metal on the back of her neck, made her feel like she was ready to jump at any moment. Did she open the door and make a run for it? The gun was too close. The smart thing was to trust the woman's word, depart, and then land, but Clarissa had spent time with her, could produce evidence against her, so she was highly likely not to survive the next two hours. Having swapped seats with Clarissa, the woman now put the gun at the head of the pilot.

'Get this bird fired up,' the woman shouted. Once again, the man didn't flinch. 'Did you hear me?' she shouted, and drove the barrel of the handgun onto his head. The man's head dropped forward, unable to lift itself back up.

The woman gasped, realizing that the pilot had been knocked out but before she could do anything, the door of the helicopter was opened and she felt herself being grabbed by the neck and tumbled out of the rear of it. As the woman's head hit the ground, and her legs collapsed around her, Hope McGrath put her hand on her wrist, twisting it hard until the gun fell from it. After that she drove down with a knee to the stomach before then spinning the woman over. She took an arm and placed a cuff on it, before cuffing the second wrist as well.

'Now, get the staff,' shouted Argyle to his man. 'Get the staff.' The door of the helicopter was opened, and Clarissa was caught holding the staff when the henchman of Lord Argyle grabbed it. He pulled hard, so hard that Clarissa fell out of the helicopter with it, hanging on as tight as she could. When she looked up, Ross had jumped up behind the man, was kicking him in the back of the knees taking him to the ground. Within twenty seconds, the henchman had his hands cuffed behind his back.

Clarissa stepped forward, her hand still in the plastic tie they've been in for the last number of hours. Macleod raced to her and looking like he was about to apologize, he suddenly wrapped his arms around her, giving her a hug.

'It's okay, we got you. We got you.'

'I'm sorry, Inspector, but it moved so quick.'

'It doesn't matter, we got you and we got him as well.' From the floor, Lord Argyle was looking up. The blood still running out of his temple, but his eyes were fixed on the Rod of Aaron, in Clarissa's hands. 'Here,' said Macleod, taking the Rod and throwing it over to him. 'Seems to be a fake to me'. Argyle used it to stand up, and with that came up to the Inspector, pointing at him.

'Heathen,' he shouted. 'Heathen.'

'You've gone mad, sir,' said Macleod. 'Heathen from the Isle of Lewis; they'll never hear of it.'

Chapter 24

'I didn't think they'd let us put it in Inverness Museum,' said Macleod. 'I'm more than a little shocked at seeing the Rod behind some glass.'

'Well, they're not keeping it here permanently. It'll be moved to one of the British museums. I'm petitioning for it to stay in Scotland. After all, this is where all the drama around it happened, but we'll have to see.'

'It also seems a lot of fuss over nothing to me,' said Macleod. 'I stood there half expecting something to happen when Argyle put it up above his head, threatened me with it, but there was nothing. I mean, is it even Aaron's staff?'

'No, it's not. The date's wrong,' said Clarissa. 'I was telling you this before. It's not when something comes from that makes it valuable. It's the story around it. Now, this staff has even more story. It's been taken. It's had three murders associated with it.'

'And all very convoluted with it,' said Macleod. 'To think that a man with a metal detector goes out, finds this Rod, is actually paranoid that people are going to take it off him or scam him for it. So much so that he hires a room for two weeks to use it for less than thirty minutes, and then turns around and hands it over to one of the best scammers going.'

'Howie Lemmon's a sad figure to end up being killed, hung up in his own flat. It's horrible. I'm not used to this, working for the arts group.'

'Well, here in the murder squad, you get used to it,' said Macleod. 'I just wish Kirsten had hung on for a bit longer. She could have briefed you on what you were going to expect.'

'The move,' said Clarissa, 'by Forrest Mackenzie was sheer genius. To put it out disguised, cover it up a bit and make it an ordinary staff, and then try and flog it. Just so that he could turn around and just hand Howie Lemmon a small sum while getting some of his own cronies to pick it up, and then blag it on for serious money, it's quite breath-taking in a lot of ways. And to set up a whole auction house just for it. Quite stunning, really.'

'With the money involved, I've seen people go to worse. Did we ever find the other bidder?' asked Macleod.

'Not the buyer,' said Clarissa. 'The woman in the cells, who held me captive, the one we now know as Jeannie Baxter, she still hasn't spoken. Still won't say who her buyer was. I reckon it was overseas. Probably Middle Eastern. The way in which Lord Argyle came after it, I always thought there was something strange about the man. To be so deluded into thinking that the staff actually was a power, I reckon the other investor just recognized it for what it was, a financial goldmine. That's why he sent Jeannie Baxter in to intercept.'

'It all goes wrong,' says Macleod, 'and she ends up having to kill people to try and get it. Then when she does get it and tries to hand it over, it all falls apart again because she doesn't even understand who her own contact is. If you hadn't wandered in at that car park, we would have been in trouble. It would have been gone.'

'If I hadn't wandered in at that car park, you wouldn't have had to come running after me. I wouldn't have had a gun at my head. I'm sorry, Inspector. I overstepped the mark on that one. You did tell me to wait.'

'If I had thought you had overstepped the mark, we would not be standing here in an Inverness Museum, discussing this. You'd be standing in front of my desk, and you'd be getting the short end of it. You did what any good officer would have done. You tailed the suspect. Then when it emerged that what was happening meant we were going to lose the case, you intervened. Yes, possibly more recklessly than I would have, but at the end of the day, it was brave. That's what I like about you, you cut to the core, you just go right after it, don't you? Do you also see it coming? You can read things.'

'Ross told me that the constable had left—Kirsten. He said you were very fond of her; said because she could cut through things.'

'It's true, I admired her work. She was very much on the same wavelength, but understand this, Clarissa, she could also stand in front of me and handle any number of people coming. She was a mixed martial artist. Good to have around a doddery old fool like me.'

Clarissa laughed and she put her purple scarf over her shoulder, turning away from the exhibit. 'Can I treat you to a drink, Inspector?'

'I already told you, I don't.'

'It's fine,' she said. 'I'll buy two, have them both. You must like coffee. That office positively stinks of it.'

'Well, if you follow me,' said Macleod, 'we'll head onto one of the old traditions we have. When we wrap up a case, especially if it's been one like this, we take time, time to look back, celebrate, bring in all the small people on the side, the ones that do all the leg work.'

'Did you read that in the manual somewhere?' Clarissa asked.

'No. That's why Hope is my sergeant. She knows that side. She gets people, she gets what they need, gets to know how to bring a team together. She sits on the top, the team work underneath her, and the only one above her is me. It gives me room to think, room to plan what we're doing. That's how the team works, Clarissa. Do you see that?'

'Well, you don't have her subtleness, Seoras. I could say that for you.'

'But you do, you handle people as well. What you did on the boat, getting on board to take the guy down below, finding out what was really happening when all he wanted to do was keep you at bay, that was smart.'

'Well, I've played parts all my life. You don't know the number and names I'm going by in the art world. In fact, I'm struggling to remember them all.'

'Well, I just want you to be plain old Clarissa Urquhart.' Macleod suddenly realized he dropped a clanger.

'Plain old Clarissa Urquhart? Yes, I can see why you have Hope to marshal the troops together,' Clarissa laughed. 'It's okay, I come from that time, too. I say it, but I say it in the right place. It's not easy to change, Seoras, is it? I come from a time when men held the door open for you. These days, I have to get offended by it. I get abuse for not promoting feminism when I like a man to wine me and dine me. I like the door held open. I like all those little touches. I hate a lot of what went on with it, the men who thought they owned their women, but the men who respected you in that way, they were good men like you.'

'I'm probably being quite long-winded about this but listen, Clarissa, this team could probably do with a little bit of old school on it, a little bit more than me. We could do with someone who can make their way into places, things on the quiet. I don't have people who can do undercover now. Kirsten was learning, but in you, I've got an old hand. Sorry, an expert.'

'Can you just say it? You want me to join your team, don't you?'

'If you want to. It's the murder squad. When people were getting killed, when you had a gun to you, those things are not that uncommon. You'll see a lot of blood; you'll see a lot of nastiness. If you can live with that, you do get to work with some exceptional people, especially the sergeants and constables. But it does mean you end up reporting to Hope. At your age and being a sergeant, to talk to a junior like that—I'm sorry I can't make it any other way, but she's there for a reason.'

'Look, Inspector, my artwork covers are blown. I can sit behind a desk, I can do all the paper chasing, I can even do the occasional stakeouts, but I can't do what I used to do. I can't waltz in and be a policewoman hiding in front of everyone. Maybe it's time for a change but you understand, I'm not the best with orders.'

'Good,' said Macleod, 'because we need a bit of that. Too many of my people will look for me, look for what I do. It's time they saw that somebody else can handle it.'

Clarissa turned around, holding out her hand and very politely shook Macleod's when he offered it. 'I take it my desk is the one opposite Ross? I might have to put a little décor in the room, you do realize that?'

'You could take that up with your boss, but you aren't touching my office.' Macleod gave a wry smile. 'Around the corner, two doors down, you'll see Hope in the pub already. Tell her I want a latte.' Clarissa nodded and turned, and Macleod watched the woman walk away. Yes, she was older but she was elegant, self-assured, and he saw the determination inside. When she had the gun held to her, she'd managed to keep her composure despite thinking she was going to be dead.

Macleod stepped outside the museum, took a walk over a grassy slope, and looked down to the River Ness flowing through the town. The sun was up. People were milling about through the city as if nothing had ever happened, and to them, it hadn't. It was just another murder far up in Invershin. A strange thing, but then again, strangers had come in. A new build, a new auction house. Maybe the public would write it off quite quickly, but what fascinated Macleod was The Order of St. Columba's Knights. How did people of such high breeding, people who had such access to knowledge, how did they come up with such a crazy notion? As Macleod stood there, he became aware that time was passing, and when someone tapped him on his shoulder, he knew exactly who it would be.

'What did she say then?'

'Yes. She said yes, but she also said that she wouldn't stick to the rules.'

'Well, you're not going to like that, are you?' said Hope.

'Not my problem. She might be a sergeant but she's under you. It's up to you how you handle her, but I warn you, she'll be more dogged than Kirsten ever was and she'll be more bloody-minded.'

'Is that a problem, sir?' asked Hope.

'That's exactly the reason I hired her. You need to learn from her, Hope. You need to stick to your guns at times. I was wrong on this one. I thought I'd take her on board and vet her, bring her onto my team. That should have been your job. I'm sorry, but you've got her now, whether you like or not.'

'She'll do simply fine,' said Hope, raising her hand up onto Macleod's shoulder. 'You miss Kirsten though, don't you? As much as Clarissa's older—'

'Careful.'

'More mature, seasoned.'

'The word you're looking for is experienced, Hope. The rest just makes me sound ancient.'

'Experienced. It'll be good to have that experience around. Kirsten was very green.'

'By the way, how's the new man?' asked Macleod.

'I'll tell you when I see him. You have us running around again. I still struggle with this job. You never see the people you're meant to be close to.'

'Or you can give him Jane's number. She's set up a commiseration club.'

'Is that what it is? A life with us, just commiserations when you don't see us enough?'

'I don't know. I was never on that side.'

'Tell me something, Seoras. That Rod—did you ever believe it was the real thing?'

'It depends what you mean by the real thing. Clarissa was on about this and it's only just hit me. The whole idea of what makes it is the rumour, the talk around it, not what it actually is.'

'But you always talk about your faith. You always say it is what keeps you going. Surely, Lord Argyle had faith in that staff.'

'He didn't have faith, Hope. He had hunger, hunger for the power. Faith happens when there's no power to be had. Faith happens when it all falls apart, when you're unsure, when you don't know.'

'But you were quite sure. You stood in front of him when he was ready to wield the staff.'

'He had a trinket, and for trinkets, people will pay vast money. We started with an auction house. I've never been in one in my life. I don't see the point. A thing has its value. Therefore, pay the value.'

'This bluffing swagger where you build it up, it made me think about Clarissa's bluff and swagger. I mean, that's why you said we're hiring her. To go undercover, to do that.'

'You call it bluff and swagger. Take note and learn. She's trodden the boards for a long time, Hope. Everything she does is practiced, with ease. Understand, she's on the team for you. There isn't that much she can teach me.' Macleod heard the long, deep sigh and was about to turn around and tell Hope how good she was at everything, how good this was, how well she could handle people, and all he was doing was going to give her extra strings to her bow, but she was gone. Well, it's like he said to Clarissa, Hope's there to deal with the people. He was just there to work out what was going on.

Read on to discover the Patrick Smythe series!

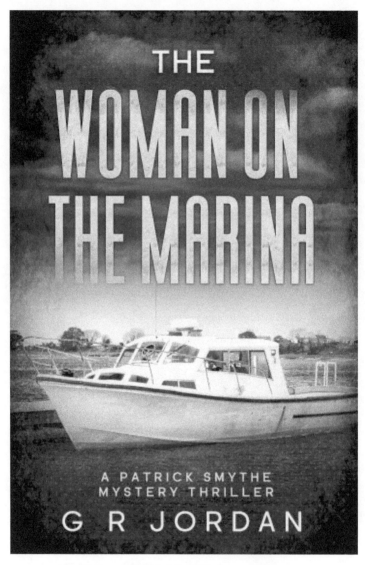

Start your Patrick Smythe journey here!

Patrick Smythe is a former Northern Irish policeman who after suffering an amputation after a bomb blast, takes to the sea between the west coast of Scotland and his homeland to ply his trade as a private investigator. Join Paddy as he tries to work to his own ethics while knowing how to bend the rules he once enforced. Working from his beloved motorboat 'Craigantlet', Paddy decides to rescue a drug mule in this short story from the pen of G R Jordan.

Join G R Jordan's monthly newsletter about forthcoming releases and special writings for his tribe of avid readers and then receive your free Patrick Smythe short story.

Go to https://bit.ly/PatrickSmythe for your Patrick Smythe journey to start!

About the Author

GR Jordan is a self-published author who finally decided at forty that in order to have an enjoyable lifestyle, his creative beast within would have to be unleashed. His books mirror that conflict in life where acts of decency contend with self-promotion, goodness stares in horror at evil, and kindness blindsides us when we at our worst. Corrupting our world with his parade of wondrous and horrific characters, he highlights everyday tensions with fresh eyes whilst taking his methodical, intelligent mainstays on a roller-coaster ride of dilemmas, all the while suffering the banter of their provocative sidekicks.

A graduate of Loughborough University where he masqueraded as a chemical engineer but ultimately played American football, Gary had worked at changing the shape of cereal flakes and pulled a pallet truck for a living. Watching vegetables freeze at -40'C was another career highlight and he was also one of the Scottish Highlands "blind" air traffic controllers. These days he has graduated to answering a telephone to people in trouble before telephoning other people to sort it out.

Having flirted with most places in the UK, he is now based in the Isle of Lewis in Scotland where his free time is spent between raising a young family with his wife, writing, figuring out how to work a loom and caring for a small flock of chickens. Luckily, his writing is influenced by his varied work and life experience as the chickens have not been the poetical inspiration he had hoped for!

You can connect with me on:

🌐 https://grjordan.com

📘 https://facebook.com/carpetlessleprechaun

Subscribe to my newsletter:

✉ https://bit.ly/PatrickSmythe

Also by G R Jordan

G R Jordan writes across multiple genres including crime, dark and action adventure fantasy, feel good fantasy, mystery thriller and horror fantasy. Below is a selection of his work. Whilst all books are available across online stores, signed copies are available at his personal shop.

The Coach Bomber (Highlands & Islands Detective Book 14)
An airport coach blown apart. A full passenger load gives a vast list of suspects. With mounting media pressure to name a killer, can Macleod dig deep into a gang war to find a deadly hitman?

When an airport bus is blown apart on the main road out of Inverness, DI Macleod finds a press backlash when they name their own suspect. With the undercurrent of an ongoing drug war upping the ante, Macleod must rely on his Sergeant Hope McGrath to infiltrate the organisations and help bring the real killer to the light.

Don't miss your stop on the way to boomtown!

Corpse Reviver (A Contessa Munroe Mystery #1)

https://grjordan.com/product/corspe-reviver

A widowed Contessa flees to the northern waters in search of adventure. An entrepreneur dies on an ice pack excursion. But when the victim starts moonlighting from his locked cabin, can the Contessa uncover the true mystery of his death?

Catriona Cullodena Munroe, widow of the late Count de Los Palermo, has fled the family home, avoiding the scramble for title and land. As she searches for the life she always wanted, the Contessa, in the company of the autistic and rejected Tiff, must solve the mystery of a man who just won't let his business go.

Corpse Reviver is the first murder mystery involving the formidable and sometimes downright rude lady of leisure and her straight talking niece. Bonded by blood, and thrown together by fate, join this pair of thrill seekers as they realise that flirting with danger brings a price to pay.

When no one else takes charge, the cream must rise to the top!

Highlands and Islands Detective Thriller Series
https://grjordan.com/
product/waters-edge
Join stalwart DI Macleod and his burgeoning new DC McGrath as they look into the darker side of the stunningly scenic and wilder parts of the north of Scotland. From the Black Isle to Lewis, from Mull to Harris and across to the small Isles, the Uists and Barra, this mismatched pairing follow murders, thieves and vengeful victims in an effort to restore tranquillity to the remoter parts of the land.

Be part of this tale of a surprise partnership amidst the foulest deeds and darkest souls who stalk this peaceful and most beautiful of lands, and you'll never see the Highlands the same way again

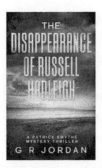

The Disappearance of Russell Hadleigh (Patrick Smythe Book 1)

https://grjordan.com/product/the-disappearance-of-russell-hadleigh

A retired judge fails to meet his golf partner. His wife calls for help while running a fantasy play ring. When Russians start co-opting into a fairly-traded clothing brand, can Paddy untangle the strands before the bodies start littering the golf course?

In his first full novel, Patrick Smythe, the single-armed former policeman, must infiltrate the golfing social scene to discover the fate of his client's husband. Assisted by a young starlet of the greens, Paddy tries to understand just who bears a grudge and who likes to play in the rough, culminating in a high stakes showdown where lives are hanging by the reaction of a moment. If you love pacey action, suspicious motives and devious characters, then Paddy Smythe operates amongst your kind of people.

Love is a matter of taste but money always demands more of its suitor.

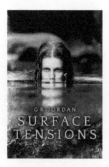

Surface Tensions (Island Adventures Book 1)
https://grjordan.com/product/surface-tensions
Mermaids sighted near a Scottish island. A town exploding in anger and distrust. And Donald's got to get the sexiest fish in town, back in the water.

"Surface Tensions" is the first story in a series of Island adventures from the pen of G R Jordan. If you love comic moments, cosy adventures and light fantasy action, then you'll love these tales with a twist. Get the book that amazon readers said, "perfectly captures life in the Scottish Hebrides" and that explores "human nature at its best and worst".

Something's stirring the water!